ST°

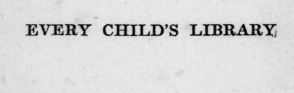

EVERY CHILD'S LIBRARY

MUX CLIMBED UP BEHIND HIS CHAIR, THREW BOTH HIS ARMS
AROUND MR. HELLMUT'S NECK AND SHOUTED HIS
THANKS RIGHT INTO HIS EARS.

CORNELLI
HER CHILDHOOD

By

JOHANNA SPYRI

Author of "Heidi," "Maxa's Children,"
"Uncle Titus in the Country,"
"A Little Swiss Boy," "Moni,
The Goat Boy."

Translated by
CLEMENT W. COUMBE

Illustrated by
FRANCES BRUNDAGE

THE
SAALFIELD PUBLISHING COMPANY
AKRON, OHIO   NEW YORK

Made in U. S. A.

FULL-PAGE ILLUSTRATIONS

Page

CORNELLI
HER CHILDHOOD

CHAPTER I

BY THE RUSHING ILLERBACH

SPRING had come and once more the young
beech trees beside the rushing Illerbach were a
tender green.   A strong south wind was swaying their branches to and fro and one moment
the bright leaves were sparkling in the sunshine, only to darken the next, for the wind kept
driving great clouds across the sun.

A little rosy-cheeked girl came running
through the grove with hair flying and eyes
sparkling with joy as first she was driven before
the wind and then fought her way against it.
From her arm dangled a hat which was
swinging back and forth and as she skipped and
ran, it threatened to tear itself from the ribbon
ties and fly away.   Soon there was a lull and as
it became more quiet the little girl began to
sing:

"Snow on the meadow,
Snow on the tiles,
Snow all around us,
Life is all smiles.
Hurrah! Hurrah!
Life is all smiles.

"The sun's in the heavens;
O birds, start your song;
Flowers by the brookside,
Let's hurry along.
Hurrah! Hurrah!
Let's hurry along.

"The swallows' returning,
The birds singing gay,
Proclaim that the springtime
Is now on the way.
Hurrah! Hurrah!
Is now on the way."

She sang with such a strong, full voice that it resounded through the whole grove and soon all the birds started to chirp and sing as though vying with her. The little girl laughed aloud in her delight and repeated as loudly as she could:

"Hurrah! Hurrah!
Let's hurry along."

and it seemed as if all the birds joined with her in one great woodland chorus.

CORNELLI, HER CHILDHOOD

At the edge of the wood stood an old beech tree with a great tall trunk. The child often sought rest in the cool shadow of its wide-spreading branches after romping about in the hot sun. She reached the tree now and stood

under it, looking up at its great swaying branches. Up above where the wind struck the open spaces it blew as strong as ever and its loud roaring in the treetops seemed to urge her to new exertions and activity. She tried to run against the wind but it was too strong, and suddenly she turned and, driven by it, raced down the steep meadow path that led into the narrow valley. She did not pause but kept on running until she reached a little cottage built on the high bank of the rushing stream where it stood looking down from its green perch on the racing torrent. Narrow steps led up to the tiny veranda about which was a wide railing. On this railing stood a great many pots of beautiful carnations. It made a lovely border around the little porch and the fragrance of the flowers was wafted afar.

It was quite evident that the little girl was very familiar with the place for she ran nimbly up the steps and dashed across the veranda.

"Martha! Martha!" she called through the open door. "Do come out! Have you noticed what a jolly time the wind is having today?"

A little old woman with gray hair and wearing a tight fitting hood stepped out. She was very simply dressed but was so neat and tidy that one might suppose she had been sitting on a chair all day long, so unruffled was her dress, though her labor-hardened hands told another story.

CORNELLI, HER CHILDHOOD

"Oh, you should see how wonderful the wind is and how it is blowing through the trees up on the hill, Martha!" the child cried excitedly. "It is blowing so hard I had to fight with all my might to keep from being blown right up in the air like a bird or to keep from tumbling down the hill. Oh, I wish you knew how jolly it is to be out in the wind!"

"I believe I would rather not experience that," said Martha as she took the child's hand in welcome. "You look as though the wind had blown you about considerably. Come, Cornelli, and I will straighten you up again."

Her thick dark hair was all tousled; what belonged on the right side of the parting was blown to the left and the hair on the left side was tossed over to the right. Instead of being in front, her pinafore hung at her side and the trimming on her jacket which had torn loose dragged along with it several twigs of thorn and leaves all in a tangle. First Martha brushed her hair and drew the apron into position, then she brought needle and thread and began to mend the torn jacket.

"Stop, Martha! Stop!" cried Cornelli, pulling away her jacket. "Your finger is all pricked to pieces! See, the needles have pricked half of it away!"

"That does not matter; let me finish your jacket," replied Martha, continuing her work. "It is not on such things that my finger is so pricked. That comes from working on the coarse shirts that I make for the peasants and the men in the iron works. It is quite different stitching into such coarse material and it is on that kind of work that I prick my finger so badly."

"You should not do that, Martha. They can make their own shirts and prick their own fingers!" cried Cornelli indignantly.

"No, no, Cornelli," objected the little old lady. "Don't you see that I am happy and thankful to get the work and so earn my daily bread? I am very thankful to the dear Lord for all the good things He gives me, and especially that I am still able to work and keep my strength."

"He really has not given you so very much, Martha," remarked the child. "You keep everything so neat and clean that your home is very pleasant—but you do all that *yourself*."

"Well, Cornelli," returned Martha, "I also thank the dear Lord that I am able to do that.

CORNELLI, HER CHILDHOOD

For you see if the good Lord did not give me the health to do all my work, who would do it for me the way I want it done? And what a wonderful gift it is to be able to step out into the lovely sunshine and linger over my carnations every morning! There, I believe I hear the bell at the foundry ringing. You know that means it is time for the master's supper; you must run across quickly."

Martha knew very well why she called her little friend's attention to returning home; only too often the time was forgotten and her father had to send for her. But now Cornelli ran down the short slope to the rushing stream until she reached the big buildings in which the crackling of fire and pounding and hammering could be heard the whole day long and only the rushing Illerbach was able to drown the noise. Cornelli glanced toward the great gates and seeing them closed, hurried on to a house that stood alone well above the stream and surrounded on three sides by well-kept flower gardens. The owner of the iron works lived here.

Cornelli ran across the lawn and into the house. Flinging her hat in a corner, she stepped into the room where her father already sat at

table holding a great newspaper before him; he did not look up. Quickly she ate her soup which was waiting for her and as her father did not even move behind his paper, she served herself through the balance of the meal.

As Cornelli was nibbling at an apple, her father looked up and said, "Well, I see you have caught up with me and, in fact, are almost through. But you must not be late for your meals; it is not proper, even though you do finish before I do. Now, if you are through, carry this letter to the post office for me. There is something in it concerning you which should please you. Tonight I shall tell you all about it."

Cornelli took the letter her father held out to her, and grasping her apple in the other hand, ran out of the house and now, skipping along beside the raging Iller, she followed the narrow valley path until it brought her to the wide highroad. Here stood the stately inn which was also the post office. In the open doorway stood the robust wife of the innkeeper and she smiled a friendly welcome as the little girl came up.

"How far? How far are you going at that double-quick pace?" she asked.

"Only to you," answered Cornelli, a little out of breath. "I have to mail a letter."

"Yes? Well, give it to me; I will take care of it for you," said the woman, and taking the little girl's hand which had been extended in greeting, she added, "You are always so happy, Cornelli; you haven't a care in the world, have you? Why don't you come oftener, for it gives me real pleasure to see such a gay and happy child as you."

Cornelli promised to do so and she meant it,

for the woman was always very kind to her. Now she said good-bye and ran gayly down the road again.

The contents of the letter that Cornelli had brought to be mailed were as follows:

"Illerbach, April 28th.

Dear Cousin:

My trip to Vienna, which I have been putting off for a whole year, must be made in the near future. I would ask a great favor of you—will you spend the summer here and superintend my household? Of course I am counting much on your good influence over my child for she has had practically no education. Miss Mina, my housekeeper, does her best, and our faithful Esther, who presides over the kitchen, also helps as much as possible. Old Martha, the nurse of my dear departed wife, has done more than anyone else, though her guidance can hardly be called an education. Of course I am to blame but I know next to nothing about bringing up little girls. Added to this, my business takes so much of my time that I seldom see the child. I know of no greater misfortune for a child than the loss of its mother. And such a mother as my Cornelia was! It was a great catastrophe for my poor child to lose her mother at the tender age of three!

It would be well to bring a friend with you so

that you will not be lonely here. I am hoping to have the pleasure of your early arrival.

Your sincere cousin,
FREDERICK HELLMUT."

That same evening when Director Hellmut and his daughter were sitting together in the living-room he told her he was hoping his cousin, Miss Kitty Dorner, would come and stay at Iller-bach while he was in Vienna and that this was a happy prospect for Cornelli.

A few days later the cousin's answer arrived. It was as follows:

"B——, May 4th.

My Dear Cousin:

I am only too glad to do you a favor and have arranged matters so that I can spend the summer at your home. I am bringing my friend Elizabeth Grideelen with me as I too believe it would be very monotonous for me to stay there alone. As to the education of your child, you really need not worry for no time has yet been wasted. You know it is quite unnecessary to be so strict with children at first; this is required only when they are old enough to be influenced mentally. A little child's mind is quite passive, as you know, and up until this time I am sure Miss Mina has looked after the child's well-being. Esther, of whom you speak very highly, has also probably done all that was necessary in taking care of your daughter. Perhaps the time has now arrived when the child is in need of a proper influence in her education.

We will arrive the last week of this month for I cannot get away before that time. With kindest regards, I remain,

Your cousin,
KITTY DORNER."

"Your cousin is coming, Cornelli, and I am sure this will please you," said her father after having read the letter at the supper table. "And another lady is coming with her, so now you will have a delightful change to look forward to."

Cornelli had never heard of this relative of her father's and felt no joy at this news. She did not see how this visit of her cousin would prove a pleasant thing for her. On the contrary, she knew it would only mean many changes in the house, which was not at all to her liking. She would much prefer to have everything remain as it was; she desired nothing else.

Cornelli rarely saw her father except at meals for he spent all his time in his business office and in the extensive foundry. However, this did not

cause the little girl to feel lonesome or forsaken.
She had so many things to do that there was not
a moment in which to be idle. The time between
school hours was always too short and the
evenings were not half long enough. Now as
soon as her father left the room, she darted out
of the house and down the path as usual.

The energetic Esther was coming up from the
garden carrying a huge basket of vegetables on
her arm for use the next day. "Don't go out,
Cornelli; look at the threatening clouds above
the mountain. I am sure we will have a storm."

"Oh, I must go to see Martha for I have something I want to tell her right away," insisted
Cornelli, "and I don't think the storm will come
very soon."

"Oh my, no! Not for a long while," called
out Miss Mina who had overheard Esther's
warning through the open door and now stepped
out. "Just run along, Cornelli; you will easily
get to Martha's before the storm breaks."

Cornelli reached Martha's cottage, ran up the
steps and burst into the little room, exclaiming,
"Just think, Martha! There are two strange
people coming to our house—two ladies from the
city! Papa says I should feel happy but I am

not a bit for I do not even know them. Would you be glad, Martha, if two strange people came to live with you?"

"Come, sit down here by me, Cornelli," said Martha gently. "First you must get your breath. Your father surely loves these visitors who are coming, else he would not expect you to be glad. And I am sure you will be very glad when you have come to know them."

"Well, perhaps; but what are you writing, Martha? I have never seen you write before."

"Writing is a difficult task for me," replied Martha. "You could do it much better than I for it is so long since I have written anything."

"Well, just tell me what to write and I will do it for you," offered Cornelli, taking the pen and dipping it to the bottom of the inkwell.

"I will tell you about it and then you write as you think best for you can word it so much better than I," said Martha, much relieved for she had been sitting for some time trying to think of a suitable beginning but quite unable to do so.

"You see, Cornelli," began the little old lady, "I have gotten along so nicely with my work lately that I am now able to carry out a plan I have long had in mind. I have been able to buy a bed and as I already had a table, an old wardrobe and two chairs, I have put all in my little room upstairs. You must come and look at them. Now I could take in someone for the summer; you know many delicate ladies and children leave the city and come to the country in the summertime. I could take good care of them for I am always at home and could be working at the same time. That is what I want to write and put in the paper, but I do not know what to say or how to begin."

"I'll put it so clearly that someone will come right away," declared Cornelli eagerly. "But first let us look at the little room; I am so anxious to see how it looks."

Martha led the way up the narrow stairway and opened the door of the little chamber.

"Oh, how lovely and neat!" exclaimed Cornelli, filled with admiration as she ran from one corner of the room to another. Martha really had arranged her little room so that it could not fail to please the most critical. The two small windows were framed with soft white curtains flowered in blue, and she had transformed an old wooden chest into a dainty washstand which also was covered with the same kind of material. The bed and two very ancient chairs were likewise covered and the room presented a most cheerful atmosphere.

"Oh Martha, how very, very lovely!" repeated Cornelli. "But how did you ever do it? It must have cost lots of money!"

"Oh no, not much. I only had to buy the bed and this material. It was a remnant and so I bought it very cheap. Do you really like it, Cornelli? Do you believe anyone would care to live in it?" asked Martha, looking critically at each separate object upon which she had worked with such care.

"Oh, yes, Martha, I know they would," Cornelli assured her. "I should love to come if I did not already live here. Now I will go down and write the notice at once for I know exactly what to say." She quickly ran down the stairs and, seating herself at the little table, dipped her pen anew and began to write the notice with great enthusiasm.

"Do not forget to give the direction and to say it is out in the country, so they can find me," reminded Martha.

"Oh, yes, I must say that too," agreed Cornelli, as she wrote the conclusion. "There, now I'll read it to you, Martha, and you can see if I have said everything."

> "If anyone wants a neat room, it can be had with Martha Wolf. She will care for delicate ladies and children who want a pleasant home. Everything is dainty and decorated with blue and white coverings. It is in the country, in Illerbach, on the Illerbach and not far from the great iron works."

Martha was quite satisfied. "You have said it all so plainly that anyone can easily understand it," said she. "I could not have written it so well myself; it sounds almost boastful. Now if I only knew to what newspaper I should send it!"

"I know just what to do," declared Cornelli. "Often when I take letters to the post office, people come in and say to the innkeeper: 'That must go into the paper.' Then he takes it and says: 'I'll attend to it.' So that's just what I'll do; give me the paper, Martha, and I will carry it to the post office."

"No, no, dear child," she objected, "I do not want you to run up there now. You have done enough for me already, but your advice is good and I will take the notice to the post office myself."

"Oh, I will go with you," insisted Cornelli

eagerly, for it was a great pleasure to take a walk with the aged Martha. She always called Cornelli's attention to such unusual things and each time would have some interesting story to relate. Many things reminded the woman of the little girl's mother, of whom she always spoke very tenderly to Cornelli and these were the only times that the child ever heard about her mother. Her father never spoke of her and when Cornelli asked Esther, who had been in their service for many years, she would always say, "Hush! Such memories only make one sad; do not think of such things."

"So you wish to come along?" asked Martha, greatly pleased, for she liked nothing better than to go for a walk with her merry little companion.

Cornelli hung on her arm and together the two wandered out into the evening air. The storm clouds had passed and the setting sun had painted the sky with a flaming gold.

"Do you think, Martha, that my mother can see the beautiful sunset from the other side as well as we can see it from this side?" asked the child, pointing to the glowing sky.

"Yes, yes, Cornelli, to be sure," declared

Martha. "If the dear God lights up the heavens so beautifully on the outside, how much more He would on the inside where all the good and blessed are rejoicing."

"But why do they rejoice?" Cornelli wanted to know.

"Oh, because they are now free from all pain and sorrow," explained Martha, "and because they know that all the pain and suffering of their loved ones here on earth is but a means to bring them to prayer and to lead them along the path to Heaven."

"And did my mother pray to Him?" asked Cornelli.

"Yes indeed, my child; you may be quite sure of that," replied Martha. "Your mother was such a good, pious lady, and we should pray that some day we may join her in Heaven."

By this time they had reached the post office and delivered their advertisement to the inn-keeper. Then they wandered back again along the pleasant valley path between the green meadows in the fast fading twilight.

CHAPTER II

ON THE TOP FLOOR

ONE bright May morning a portly gentleman who leaned heavily on a gold-headed cane was walking up a narrow city street. The houses were so high that the upper windows could scarcely be seen, the passersby having to walk so near to the buildings. From time to time the gentleman had to stop to get his breath for there was a steep grade to the street. He closely scanned the numbers on the house-doors and each time exclaimed to himself, "Not even yet!" Continuing his climb, he finally came to the desired number. The front door stood open, disclosing six bell-buttons on the entry wall. Carefully studying the names inscribed beneath each one, he shook his head until he came to the last. "Ah, here it is at last! And the very topmost!" He sighed deeply as he began the strenuous climb up the narrow stairs.

At first the stairway, though steep, was well lighted and looked very neat; then it became darker and narrower and at last ended in uneven, well-worn steps leading directly to a narrow door. There was no landing and one had to reach the door from the top step. "It is but a cage!" said the climber, panting and holding on to the wooden railing for the thin, creaking stairs seemed very unsteady to him. He pulled

the bell-rope and the door was opened by a lady in black.

"Ah, it is you, my kind counselor!" she exclaimed in surprise. "I am indeed sorry you had to climb up all these stairs," she added, seeing that he was quite out of breath and was mopping his face. "I would gladly have come down to you if you had let me know you were here," and by her gesture invited him to step in and be seated.

"As your lawyer I simply had to pay you one visit," said the gentleman, seating himself on an old sofa and still supporting himself by placing both hands on the golden knob of his cane. "I must tell you, Mrs. Halm, that I am very sorry you moved into the city instead of taking a small house in the country. That would have been a great deal more practical and convenient than to live in an undesirable attic."

"I could not think of my own convenience when I lost my husband and had to leave the parsonage, Mr. Schaller," replied Mrs. Halm with a feeble smile. "The country air would certainly have been better for my children but my eldest boy goes to school in the city and to let him go away from me, delicate as he is, would have been impossible. Besides—"

"There are boarding-houses in the city where such children are well taken care of," interrupted the gentleman. "What other reasons did you have?"

"My girls too are old enough to learn some

occupation by which they may later earn a livelihood and you know how necessary that is. You must realize that it is very difficult to obtain such opportunities in the country and so I hope you will agree with me that it was a better plan to bring the children with me to the city. I am very glad to have this opportunity of explaining why I did not follow your advice."

"And what are your daughters going to study?" asked the lawyer rather abruptly.

"Nika, the elder, paints quite well," answered the widow, "and Agnes has a decided gift for music. So I thought if both girls study earnestly, they would later be able to teach."

"These arts take endless years of study and then the returns are far from satisfactory," said Mr. Schaller practically. "It would be far better if they devoted their time to ladies' tailoring. It would not take so long to learn that and then, working together, the two could open a business in the near future. I am sure this plan would be a great deal more beneficial to you and your son, for if he is to finish his studies he will not be self-supporting for some time."

The widow gazed sadly before her, but said never a word.

"Please do not misunderstand me, Mrs. Halm," continued the gentleman, "for I am advising you only for your own interest and that of your children. I am very sorry I did not meet your daughters for I am sure they would have agreed with me after hearing my reasons."

"Perhaps my children have been influenced by their parents in this respect and will not care to give up the things you call breadless arts," said the widow with a sigh. "However, I will inform my children of your views insofar as I am able."

"What is the age of your eldest daughter?" asked Mr. Schaller. "She ought to be old enough to realize my views are the most practical."

"Nika is now in her fourteenth year," replied Mrs. Halm, "and so you may know her education is still incomplete. Dino is twelve and Agnes eleven and must still finish her legal school period."

"Still quite young," said their guardian, shaking his head. "One thing is certain, however, as their educations are yet far from complete: we must find the shortest way to reach the goal for which they are striving. I am becoming more and more convinced that my suggestion is a good one and that your daughters should be apprenticed to an expert ladies' tailor so that your moving to the city will not have been in vain."

In his eagerness to convince his quiet listener, Mr. Schaller had not noticed a little youngster who stepped in, first to hide behind his mother and then at her sign to approach the gentleman. Not until a small fist was forced into his half-closed hand was he aware of the little newcomer.

"Well, well! Here is another, the smallest! And what is your name, my little man?"

"Mux," was the prompt reply.

Mr. Schaller looked inquiringly at the mother.

"That is the name the children gave him and which for some unaccountable reason we all still use. His correct name is Markus and he has just passed his fifth year."

"I see! And what are you going to be when you grow up, my little friend?" asked the gentleman kindly.

"A cavalry general," answered the little fellow without hesitation.

Mr. Schaller now arose and said impressively, "Mrs. Halm, it seems that all your children have rather high notions in their heads. I only hope they will learn in time that in this world it is not always possible to do the things one likes but that we must do the things most suited to our needs."

The widow agreed on this point and added, "But I must tell you that little Mux has decided upon this because of a picture in his favorite book showing a general on horseback that has so interested him. This fancy will pass away like all other childish notions."

"You cannot impress on the young mind the proper vocation too early or too often, Mrs. Halm. You must not forget that." And with these words Mr. Schaller bade her good-bye and began to descend the steep stairs.

At that moment a little girl came running up the stairs so swiftly she did not seem even to touch the steps. As the gentleman took the whole width of the stairway the little girl was about to slip under his arm which he stretched out to grasp the railing when he lowered it to obstruct the way and said, "Stop! stop! Do you not belong to the widow, Mrs. Halm?"

"Yes, I am her daughter," was the quick response, and, bending still lower, she tried once more to pass.

"Just wait a minute, if you can," commanded the gentleman. "I am Lawyer Schaller, your mother's legal adviser, and have just been giving her some good advice concerning you. You do not look at all stupid and must help to persuade your mother for I am sure you will understand what is best for you all. Are you the elder girl?"

"No, I'm the younger," was the quick reply.

"All the better!" he said. "The elder will be even more reasonable and I am sure both of you will follow my advice for the good of the entire family." With these words he gave the child his hand and continued on his way.

Agnes darted up the rest of the stairs and into the narrow passage. Little Mux stood expectantly at the open door as was his wont every day when it was time for the children to come home for he greatly loved the hubbub and gayety that followed the silent morning.

"There was a fat gentleman here!" he announced. "And after he went mother said, 'O God!' And you cannot play the piano any more."

Agnes ran into the next room and then out again. "Where is mother? Mother! Mother!"

"Here I am, Agnes, but do not be so noisy and excited," called her mother from the kitchen.

Agnes ran out to her. "Mother, is what Mux is saying really true? I know that Mr. Schaller has been here and that he can say what we must do. What did he tell you? Is Mux right? If he is, I'd rather never do anything more and never eat or sleep again. It's the end of everything!"

"No, no, child! You must not talk like that and get so excited," quietly admonished the mother. "This is no time to discuss such an important question. We had better wait until this evening. You know very well, Agnes, your wishes and ambitions mean everything to me and as soon as we have a quiet hour, we will all talk it over together."

These words calmed the girl. She knew her mother always shared every experience with them and was as eager as herself to fulfil the long-cherished desire to complete her musical education. It lay as close her mother's heart as her own, and she could safely count on her help. She went quickly about her work in the kitchen for if her mother was not to do all that work, both she and her sister must lend a hand, as their only servant was a young girl who was capable of doing little more than run errands.

Mux had gone back to his post again, immensely pleased that his words had made such an impression on Agnes and produced great agitation. He wished to repeat the experience, and hearing someone mounting the stairs, prepared his speech. Long before Nika had reached the top he began:

"There has been a fat gentleman here, and after he had gone mother said, 'O God!' and you are not to paint any more trees and flowers."

But Nika had not met Mr. Schaller and so his words had no meaning for her. Undisturbed, she passed her brother and went into the other room. Mux was much disappointed, so when he heard Dino running up the stairs, he unloaded his news on him.

"We are not going to have what you expect," he called out to the last arrival.

"What am I thinking we shall have, you little thought-reader?" his brother asked.

"Oh, I know by the way you leaped up the stairs you thought we were going to have green peas for dinner. You are so fond of them, you could scarcely wait," asserted Mux. "But we are not going to have them today. We are going to have cabbage instead. There, now you know!"

"Well, come on anyhow, and we will see who makes the worst grimaces over it, you or I!" And taking the little fellow by the hand the two hurried into the room.

Soon afterwards the family sat down to dinner, but the meal was far different from usual. Ordinarily all the children clamored to tell their experiences of the morning, and they would all talk at once so that it was difficult for the mother to listen to any one story. Today it was quiet—the calm before a storm. All the faces were heavily beclouded except one. Agnes had explained Mux's words to Nika, and now she sat brooding, looking at her plate and gulping frequently without tasting a morsel of food, as though she had enough to do to digest what was in her mind without asking her stomach to digest food. Agnes sat with knitted eyebrows, her forehead a mass of wrinkles. The mother must have been engrossed in sad thoughts, as one could see by her distressed looks. Yes, even Mux, who was most always talkative, partook of his cabbage between sighs. Dino alone looked with happy smiles from one to the other; his dinner did not seem to require much of his attention.

"I am expecting a storm," he said, as the quiet lasted. "Nika will let loose the lightning that is flashing under her eyelashes, and Agnes will follow with the thunder. Then soon the rain will begin to fall, for Mux can hardly restrain a flood of tears over this distressing cabbage."

"But you have eaten much less cabbage than I," said Mux in a plaintive tone.

"You see, my little Mux, I do that out of politeness, so that no one need go without," explained his brother.

"If I had the time I would answer you about the thunder and the cabbage, Dino," Agnes declared. "But at one o'clock I have my music lesson; and then, besides, I have enough to swallow without this cabbage."

"It would please me more, dear Dino, if your politeness extended in other directions," said the mother with a sad smile. "You are eating nothing at all today, and last night I heard you cough continually. Your health gives me great anxiety. Did you cough much in school this morning?"

"Yes, mother; but it is nothing to distress you. It will soon pass off. My professor said today it would have been better for me if I had stayed in my native village and feasted on the rich milk from the pastures than to have hunted up the dusty corners of the city, but I replied, 'But Latin does not grow in the milk-rich pastures, professor.'"

"I hope you made no such reply as that," said the mother.

"But I did, though it was only in my thoughts! You must not worry about me any more, mother," said Dino soothingly.

"I fear the professor is right," sighed the mother. "But a plan has come into my mind which we shall talk over this evening and, Nika and Agnes, we shall discuss the proposition of our adviser. Please do not look so unhappy; we have not yet lost all."

"But that is what is going to happen," said Nika as she left the room.

"Yes, and even worse than that," added Agnes as she pushed her chair noisily into place, put some music in her portfolio and hurried off.

"What is worse than to lose everything?" called Dino after her.

"I know all right," said Mux knowingly, while Agnes only cast a backward look at Dino that said plainly, "If I had time I would not owe you an answer."

"What is it then, you wise little man?" asked Dino.

"If she had nothing but cabbage to eat all the time," answered Mux, convinced by his own experience of this truth.

Full of anxiety, the mother stroked Dino's thick hair. "My dear boy," she said as he rose to go, "beware of running too swiftly, will you not? It is not good for you to become overheated and then sit in the cool schoolroom. You see, I cannot have you go away any more without anxiety."

"But, mother mine, I am not so sick as all that," said Dino, tenderly embracing her. "When anyone has a cough, it always goes away again. That is the way it will be with me. Just be cheerful and everything will come out all right. Now I must run off!" he exclaimed.

"Do not hurry so much, Dino. You have plenty of time, just remember that," his mother called out after him, then she hurried to the open window and gazed down into the street to look after him.

Of all the cares she had to bear, this worry about Dino's health was the hardest, and now showed itself in the pained expression on her face as she closed the window and returned to her sewing.

Mux had put the same question to her three times without being heard. Then he raised his voice and asked the fourth time loudly, "Mama, why must we eat just what the cows do?"

"What are you talking about, Mux?"

"I saw it quite plainly in my picture book; the leaves the cows eat are the same as those in our kitchen," he explained, though not very clearly. But his mother understood him at once, for she remembered how intently he had gazed at the big head of cabbage the maid brought into the kitchen early that morning. Immediately she recalled a picture in Mux's beloved book showing the glossy brown cow being fed luscious green leaves by the stable man.

"Are you still thinking about the cabbage you do not like?" asked his mother. "That is not right, when there are so many poor children who must go hungry. You get good bread and healthful boiled vegetables."

"Then we should send them some of the cabbage we have to eat," suggested Mux quickly.

"Come, take up your sewing that I have commenced for you. We will start a working race, and so forget about the cabbage. Here, sit down by me."

The mother drew a stool nearer to her and put the sewing into the lad's hands. Now the race of stitches began, and in his eagerness to beat his mother Mux quickly forgot the cabbage which had weighed so on his mind.

Late evening arrived when all school studies were over and the mother put aside her great mending basket as usual to take up the knitting of stockings—work that did not require much attention. This was the hour when the children crowded around her to tell her the joys and sorrows of the day.

For little Mux it was the hardest time of the day for before the mother entered into conversation with the older children, she always took his hand and led him to bed.

This evening his mother must have been in a special hurry about bedtime, for before the tiny fellow was ready for the struggle he found himself in his crib and cosily tucked in for the night. Now Mux always took his fate peacefully after he had reached his cot, for then came the moment when his mother seated herself comfortably by his side so that he, just like the others, could tell her about the things that lay next his heart. Knowing that once his prayers had been said, the conversation came abruptly to an end, he aimed to delay the prayer by every possible method.

"Mama," he said thoughtfully after climbing into his crib tonight, "if one should plant cherries in all the places where cabbages now grow, then everybody could eat cherries instead of cabbage, couldn't they?"

"We will have to drop that matter, my little Mux," said his mother much to his surprise, for he had thought he could start a long conversation. "I see you cannot forget the cabbage we had for dinner today. Now you must go to sleep. You have talked about it long enough."

Mux knew nothing was to be gained, and as soon as he had finished his prayers and his mother had kissed him, he lay down and was fast asleep almost as soon as his mother had closed the door behind her.

Agnes had just finished her last lessons for school and threw her books into a drawer, each one more violently than the last. She was driven by some powerful emotion, and as soon as she saw her mother enter the room, she burst forth with, "O mother, if I may not finish my musical education, I prefer to learn nothing—absolutely nothing more! I will become a servant girl! I can do that all right and when I have earned enough money I'll buy a harp and go from house to house singing," and there followed a flood of tears which choked further words.

During this stormy speech, Nika had bent her head lower and lower over the drawing on which she toiled away without once looking up. Now pushing away the paper, she held her handkerchief to her face to wipe away the tears.

"Oh, my children, don't be so despondent!" exclaimed the mother, giving them a troubled look. "You know full well that your troubles are mine also and that I do and will continue to do all I can so you may pursue your studies as you desire. It would be my greatest joy to have you develop your talents so that your whole lives could be devoted to music and painting. But if this cannot be done, children, we must have faith to believe that it is not best for you; that the dear Lord has some other plan that must be better. Let us not lose confidence, but hold fast to the solace that the Father in Heaven guides us in love. He will not forget us. Let us also remember that He sees farther than we and knows why and where He guides us. Even though we cannot understand at the moment, some day we will find that hardship is laid upon us only to bless us."

"Now let us all be happy once again and sing a song," interrupted Dino who liked to be merry and, more than that, desired to see everyone around him gay. "Now let us sing:

> And storms the winter e'er so bad
> The spring will soon be coming.
> Though now our Agnes is so sad,
> New tunes she'll soon be humming."

"Yes, yes, Dino; it's all very well to laugh!" flared up Agnes. "But if you had to become a tailor, you would whistle another tune. *You* can study everything you want to."

"No, I really do not want to study everything—better just one thing," corrected Dino. "But I will tell you something, Agnes—your singing is much better than your reasoning; that you must acknowledge. Please begin, and if my song does not please you, strike up another one."

"We will conclude with a song, children," said the mother, "but now I have something to talk over with you, Dino. Your cough and your looks worry me, and I have been searching for some time to find a place in the country where you could spend several weeks to gain strength. There are plenty of places, of course, but I must find some modest house where someone will also take care of you. Today I found an advertisement in the newspaper and it might prove to be what I am looking for. See here, Dino; read it yourself."

Dino took the paper and read. Then he laughed aloud. "Yes, mother, I must go there," he said as he again shook with laughter. "Off to Martha on the Illerbach! It certainly must be comfortable at Martha Wolf's, where the room is so

prettily decorated and fitted out with such neat white and blue coverings."

Now the other children clamored to know how the advertisement read which had set Dino to laughing so, and he read aloud the notice of Martha Wolf of Illerbach. They all quickly agreed that Martha's most comfortable lodging must be found and the mother determined to write to the woman immediately and to send Dino there as soon as possible.

"Now, children, let us sing a hymn to close the day," she said as she seated herself at the old piano, for she always accompanied the children at the evening singing. "What would you like to sing to me tonight?" she asked as she opened her song book. Then as she struck up a tune, all three children raised their voices with:

> "When sorrow comes
>   Confide in God,
> And He will ever heed,
>   For in His love
> He'll guard you well
>   Whene'er you are in need.
> Before you ask,
>   Before you pray,
> He knows what will befall;
>   So trust in God
> And seek Him oft,
>   For He awaits your call."

CHAPTER III

THERE was great excitement in the Director's house at Illerbach. The day had come when the two ladies from the city were expected. The master had given orders for a banquet, which he wished served soon after the arrival of his two guests whom he expected about midday. He had been longing for the coming of his cousin and so now was in his best humor. It was necessary that he start on his journey immediately, but he did not think it proper to go before receiving his guests and placing the house in his cousin's care according to her expressed desire. The next day was therefore fixed for his departure.

Cornelli watched the household preparations in a mood that did not augur well for the happiness of the guests. Ordinarily she always anticipated company with joy and at such times would run into the kitchen where the baking was going on. She would scarcely cross the threshold when Esther would call out, "Come,

52

taste! Which do you like best? Though probably neither one is so bad." A small golden-
yellow apple pie and a reddish-brown plum tart
would be ready on a little plate for her, for her
visit was expected. Cornelli would pronounce
the apple pie a huge success, and the plum tart
even better than the pie.

Then Cornelli would go across into the
pantry, where Miss Mina was busy preparing
the dessert on little crystal plates. There some
blue Malaga raisins would fall off the plates,
and some almonds would also roll off, quickly
disappearing in Cornelli's pockets. She liked to
carry such a supply to eat whenever she felt like
it, and Miss Mina often let a goodly number of
almonds and raisins drop on purpose, for she
wanted to be sought after just as much as
Esther, and well knew what tempted Cornelli
into the kitchen.

Today Esther made quite a clatter with her
dishes and pans and when Cornelli came to see
what baking had been going on she called,
"Away! Away! There's nothing for you today! The ladies from the city must not think
they can show us how a good dinner is cooked.
We shall teach them. Run away, Cornelli, run

53

away! I must prepare my vegetables here!"

Cornelli ran across to the pantry.

Miss Mina was just arranging an artistic pile of cookies and almond rings. "Don't rush in here or you will upset them all," she called out to the child. "Don't come so near the table. See, one of the plates is already finished. There must be nothing amiss, for I'll not have it said by the ladies that one can quickly see there is no mistress in the house and that nobody here is able to set a table."

"If you are so stingy too, I won't bother you any more today," said Cornelli and faced about and ran away.

Just then she heard the approach of a carriage, and hurried to the front of the house to look down the road. Yes, there came the expected coach, and the two ladies in it. Cornelli called, "Matthew, Matthew!" as she hastened toward the barn and great stables that lay not far from the house, but hidden by trees. "Come, Matthew, the coach will be here in a moment!"

Matthew attended to the horses and superintended all the work in stable and garden done by the young farm hands.

He now came to the stable door and beckoned

mysteriously to her. "Come here, Cornelli! Come quick, right quick! We'll meet the coach in good time."

Cornelli ran over, and there in a corner of the stable, nicely bedded in hay, lay a little

snow-white kid. It looked like the neatest little toy, but it was actually alive.

"Oh, where did you get it, Matthew? Oh, how cunning it is! Its white fur is just like silk! Can it walk by itself? Can it stand up if it wants to? Oh, look how friendly it is, and how it lays its head on my arm!"

"Come now, come along! The coach is driving

up. You can pay it a visit every day," Matthew reminded her. "Come along quick. Just fancy, it was only born today."

Matthew was punctual and on duty as the horses pulled into the courtyard. The master appeared at the same time, for it was his nature to be polite so he had had a watch set to inform him when the carriage drew near. He handed his cousin out, greeting her heartily. Then he helped Miss Grideelen to descend, expressing his warm thanks to her for coming. He told her it was most kind of her to accompany his cousin into this solitude, and he counted it a real favor, for the thought of leaving his self-sacrificing cousin alone so long had worried him, for urgent business might make his absence longer than he could foresee.

"Where is your daughter, Frederick?" now inquired Miss Dorner.

The Director looked around. "I saw her around here just a little while ago. Where are you, Cornelli?" he called towards the house.

"Here I am!" sounded from quite close by, for Cornelli had hidden behind her father so that, without being seen, she would be able to get a good view of the new arrivals.

"Come and welcome your cousin and Miss Grideelen," her father said.

Cornelli gave her hand first to her relative and then to the other lady. "Good-day," she said both times.

"You may call me cousin, and this lady is Miss Grideelen," said Miss Dorner, expecting that the child would repeat the greeting and use the correct address, but Cornelli did not say anything further.

Mr. Hellmut had turned his attention to the carriage and was giving Matthew orders concerning the horses. Now the four entered the house and soon were seated at dinner, Miss Mina receiving warm praise for the delicious meal and the attractive table. During the afternoon Mr. Hellmut showed the ladies over his estate, for his cousin wished to learn about everything she had to watch over.

"What a wealth of vegetables!" exclaimed Miss Grideelen repeatedly. "How many cherry trees! What immense apple trees! And that splendid row of pear trees! Really, Mr. Hellmut, you must be able to fill great store rooms with fruit in the autumn! Where do you find room for it all?"

"I do not know, for the servants attend to that. I myself have no time to give to it."

"It is a pity, Frederick, that you do not have half a dozen children. They would help take care of the place," remarked the cousin. "By the way, what has become of your daughter? She does not seem very sociable."

"I do not know where Cornelli is," admitted Mr. Hellmut. "At this time of day I am usually at my work over yonder. Miss Mina knows where the child is. Perhaps her teacher is with her. The child could not well be sociable, for she is always alone. It is on this account that I am so glad and thankful that you ladies have come, for now, at last, she will have the environment I have so long wished her to have. But what could I do? Twice I have had a governess for her, to give her a companion and the proper education. But the first left because she could not stand the loneliness of our house and the second wanted me to dismiss every servant in the house: Esther was to go and Matthew too. And when I made no move to dismiss my old servants, she told me to make my choice. Either she or the 'old house-rats' must leave. I said, 'Better you, for when the other two were gone, I would be the oldest house-rat. It would be my turn next to go.' So she too journeyed off. I had no more courage to go through other similar experiences, although I knew it was high time for Cornelli to have a lady of culture and good education around her. You, cousin, will be able to give me good advice when you have become acquainted with the child."

"I would like to know whom your child looks most like," said Miss Dorner. "She bears no resemblance to you or to her mother."

"Do you think so?" asked Mr. Hellmut. "Do you really think that? I do not wish the child to look like me, but I have always hoped she would have the features of her mother as she grew older, to recall her memory to me."

Mr. Hellmut looked pleadingly at his cousin.

She shrugged her shoulders and said, "I can see no likeness in the little shaggy savage to the pretty and brilliant Cornelia. Her joy-filled eyes seemed always to laugh at one from under her waves of brown hair. Candidly, I must say, Frederick, your child is not attractive; she looks like an ill-tempered kitten, its back humped and its hair standing straight up, all ready to spring and scratch."

"No, no, the child is not like that," declared Mr. Hellmut. "She is not ill-tempered; at least I do not think so. But you are right," he continued with a sigh, "she is not like her mother. Perhaps her training or lack of training is much to blame. It is on this account that I am so thankful to you and to Miss Grideelen for coming and staying a while. Certainly under your influence and your guardianship the child will change and gain much, for I do not believe it is difficult for Cornelli to learn. Now I can travel with a light heart and can leave the child, house and servants all in your hands. You cannot know how difficult my position was when it was absolutely necessary for me to travel. There is not a soul here capable of presiding over the house with authority. I cannot thank you enough for making my present journey easy."

When the party returned from their walk, they separated, the ladies going to their rooms to arrange their belongings and Mr. Hellmut to attend to last preparations for his journey. They met again at the supper table, both guests and host appearing punctually, and the meal was served immediately.

"Where is your daughter?" inquired Miss Dorner. "Does she not come to supper?"

"Why, yes! Miss Mina, do you know where she is?" asked Mr. Hellmut.

Just then the door opened and Cornelli came in with glowing cheeks.

"Have you been creeping through a hedge?" asked Miss Dorner.

"No; I was in the hen house," answered Cornelli.

"That is quite enough to account for your appearance. You had better go to your room first and have Miss Mina put your hair to rights and apply soap where it is necessary."

Cornelli looked at her father; this was something new, and needed confirmation.

"Quick, quick, Cornelli! What are you thinking of?" he rebuked her. "You must obey your cousin; she is taking my place now. Everybody in the house must understand that," he added with a glance toward Miss Mina.

The maid started to follow the child but Cornelli called back, "I can do it myself."

When she returned, her face and hands had been carefully washed, but her hair was tossed into confusion. She had combed it so that one could not tell what belonged on one side of the part and what on the other, what belonged in front and what behind. Miss Dorner laughed. "Your head looks like a wind-blown hayfield," said she. "Miss Mina must part it properly in the morning."

CORNELLI, HER CHILDHOOD

Cornelli drew her forehead into a pucker and did not look up again from her plate during the meal.

Early the next morning Mr. Hellmut started on his journey.

The village of Illerbach, where the church and school were located, was too far from the iron foundry for Cornelli to walk there to school every day. Besides, Mr. Hellmut thought it better for her to have her lessons at home, so a teacher came every morning to instruct her in all the necessary branches. In the afternoon she was free except for the little time required to prepare her lessons for the next day. Therefore Cornelli had so far led a very free existence. She had always had plenty of time for a daily visit to her old friend Martha and they carried on absorbing conversations. She also wandered at will through the beech woods and along the whole length of the mountain. There were so many beautiful and wonderful things to search for in the woods and fields that her excursions never ended as long as the sun shone. If rain or snow prevented her tramping, then there was Martha's comfortable little cottage to serve as a lovely stopping place.

CORNELLI, HER CHILDHOOD

Her teacher had just left the house. Her father's departure that morning had afforded ample material for sentences that Cornelli had to compose in her hour's study of German, and all her answers came so pat that the teacher declared the lesson ended with the stroke of the hour. With a special word of praise for her good work of the day he bade her good-day, and Cornelli shook his proffered hand energetically, for she and the teacher were the best of friends.

Cornelli's lessons always gave the two the greatest satisfaction. The teacher knew his pupil well. When she was fresh and lively, he would make a hard drive with the work, and in no time at all they had accomplished three times as much as usual. Then he dismissed his pupil promptly at the stroke of the clock for fatigue was never allowed to spoil their pleasure. But if Cornelli was distracted and dull, he went ahead very slowly and as considerately as though she were a little weak-minded. He would continue this way until the hand of the clock showed a quarter, a half or even three quarters of an hour beyond the time set for study. This did not leave a good quarter of an hour before lunch for Cornelli to run to the garden, to the stable, to the poultry house,—something Cornelli always reckoned on. The teacher at last would stop and in saying good-bye would remark in his most friendly way, "I had to stay so long because we did not finish half of what we had to do today. You were a little slow in understanding, Cornelli. But tomorrow matters will go better; otherwise your lesson will have to last even longer."

Today Cornelli had a special incentive for working in order to gain early release. She had not been able to see the little kid since yesterday. Lessons over, she darted out to the stable. Lunch was at one o'clock; she still had an hour. Matthew had seen the child running, and called out to her, "Come, come, Cornelli! It has just jumped out."

Cornelli hurried into the stable. Correct! There the tiny snow-white kid skipped happily to and fro around its mother who was lying in the hay. Its leaps were so dainty that Cornelli was enchanted.

"You pretty little creature!" she exclaimed, stroking its silky fur. "Now I'll bring you a red neck-ribbon, and then I will take you out for a walk."

She ran back to the house, rummaged among her things and returned with a cherry-red ribbon. When this was tied around the neck of the little kid, Cornelli declared nothing was more lovely than the little creature with its white

coat and red bow. It continued to gambol about, then suddenly leaped into the hay and gazed up at Cornelli with a look of intense satisfaction.

"May I take it out, Matthew? May I take it for a walk? Can it be hitched to a little cart and be driven around?" asked Cornelli, spinning out a second new plan before Matthew had caught up with the first.

"Wait, wait; give it a chance to grow, that's

the main thing," answered Matthew prudently. "You see just now the tiny creature is like a little child that is learning to walk; it must stay near its mother, and can only run about near her. When it has grown bigger, the longer walks will come, and when it is strong, we'll harness it. Then you can take a drive, two reins in one hand and a whip in the other."

Cornelli shouted with joy and again stroked the kid tenderly, full of thoughts of the lovely drives they would have together when the time arrived.

"Did you hear the bell at the foundry? It's time for lunch. You must take care now; there are strangers managing the house," said Matthew cautiously.

Cornelli had not heard the bell through sheer joy over her new pet; but she went off at once for she had a feeling that from now on she must appear punctually at the table. She ran toward the house and as she passed the well it occurred to her she should wash her hands. She held them both under the spout and rubbed them together with energy. She then dipped her face and rubbed it too. There was no towel, so her handkerchief, though small, did duty.

"Hurry up, hurry up! The ladies are already sitting at table," sounded the warning voice of Esther from the kitchen window.

Cornelli ran in. The ladies were actually at

table, and a plate of soup was at her place awaiting her.

"You must come to your meals punctually. You can hear the bell ring very well over yonder," said Miss Dorner. "But what a sight you are! Half-wet arms, your apron all soaked, your feet damp—have you been in the water? What have you been doing?"

"I washed my hands under the well spout, and I got splashed," explained Cornelli.

"Easily understood!" remarked Miss Dorner. "But there are arrangements in your room for washing your hands and there one does not get splashed. Go, put on another apron. At table you must appear neat."

"There is something good about the child, for she obeys," remarked Miss Grideelen after Cornelli had left the room. "She always comes to her meals washed since you gave those instructions."

"That is true," admitted Miss Dorner, "but she has unheard-of habits and manners. How shall we set her on the right path? Really you must help me in the morning, Miss Mina. Above all, comb the child's hair and part it as I asked you yesterday."

"That is what I did this morning and always do every morning," replied the servant, rather wounded. "But her hair is like bristles and difficult to braid. Cornelli needs to make only one jump and it is all tangled again, and she jumps every moment."

Cornelli had come downstairs again, and had eaten her soup. Her place was next to Miss Dorner, while Miss Grideelen sat opposite.

"What is this sticking to your clothes?" asked her cousin, looking with disgust at the edge of Cornelli's skirt, from which something was hanging. "Can it be hay or straw? It certainly looks very untidy. Is it possible you have just come out of the stable?"

"Yes, I have," Cornelli replied.

"How horrid! Why, now I can smell it! That is going a little too far!" exclaimed Miss Dorner. "I am sure your father would not allow that if he knew it."

"Oh, surely he would! He goes there himself!" returned Cornelli.

"Do not answer impertinently. It is quite another matter for your father," Miss Dorner pointed out. "One thing I must tell you and you must remember it: If you are allowed to go into the stable, and you find pleasure in it, you may do so. But afterward, before you come to meals, you will go up to your room, wash yourself thoroughly and change your dress. Do not forget that! You understand?"

"Yes," assented Cornelli.

"It is strange what amusements children in the country have," remarked Miss Grideelen. "Have you no books, Cornelli? Would you not much prefer to read than to roam around and to go to the stables?"

"No indeed, I would rather not! I have enough of books," answered the child.

"What are you going to do after lunch? You have no more lessons to do," said the cousin.

"Then I will go to Martha," was the reply.

"Who is Martha?" Miss Dorner wished to know.

"A woman," said Cornelli.

"I can well believe that," remarked the cousin. "But what kind of a woman?" Then turning to Miss Mina, "What sort of a woman is she? Should the child be allowed to go to see her? Does anyone in this house know her?"

"Oh yes, she has been known here for a long time and came to the house before I did," replied

Mina. "She nursed the late mistress in her last sickness. She is a very good woman, and always appears neat and tidy. The master is very fond of her."

"Well, now we know what we are about. You really must learn to answer properly, Cornelli," said Miss Dorner. "You are like some wild hare, you do everything in leaps and bounds. You may go to see the woman, but first sit down and prepare tomorrow's lessons; surely you have some to do."

Cornelli acknowledged she had, and as soon as the ladies left the room to pass the hottest hours of the day in their bedrooms Cornelli seated herself at her little table in the corner and wrote a whole page at lightning speed. Then she seized the book and read her lesson over and over again until she knew it by heart. Next the books were tossed into a corner and Cornelli darted off.

"Oh, Martha, you ought to hear how things are going since papa left," Cornelli called out as she ran up the steps to her aged friend.

"What is the matter, Cornelli? What makes you so cross? Come, come, sit down by me a little while and tell me about it," said Martha in her friendly manner and placed a chair alongside the table where she was doing some mending and on which all the pieces lay in order.

"You cannot understand how things are," continued Cornelli with unabated excitement.

"With you everything goes along smoothly and nobody comes to give orders that everything must be different. Now I must not go inside without washing myself, and I must never come in the house from the stable without putting on another dress; and I must not wash my hands at the yard spout because it splashes. So many new things must be done, and everything is changed."

"Well, you know there is nothing bad about the fact that everything should not be just the way it was before," remarked Martha thoughtfully. "I think the lady who is related to you wishes to have things go on with you as your dear mother would have had if she had stayed with us. That is only for your good. You see, Miss Mina and Esther mean well by you, but your relative knows far better what is needed so that you will grow up as your mother would have wished. Just think how pleased your father will be if you grow to be like her and always remind him of her when he looks at you!"

Cornelli shook her head. "I can never be that," she exclaimed. "And you yourself have said mother was like no other person."

"Yes, yes, I certainly did say that!" acknowledged Martha, "but let me explain something to you, Cornelli. If you cannot be exactly as your mother was, you can be the very next thing to being like her—much more so than anyone else. For you are her child, and a child always inherits something from the mother. Sometimes you can give one a look like she did, with the same brown eyes; though not when your fore-head is all wrinkled up in frowns like today. You must pay close attention to the way the ladies do, how they act and the way they speak. They are of the same class and kind as your mother, and that is why I am so pleased that you can watch their ways and make them your own. Then in act and manner you can be like your mother."

"Indeed, I will do just what you think best," responded the child willingly, "but I'm not a bit glad that they are here and everything has to be so different. Oh, now a thought has just occurred to me. I must run off immediately. Just think of it, Martha, at this time of day I always went to gather apples and cherries and whatever was ripe in the orchards. That is the place such things taste best. But now I must always sit at table punctually at five o'clock, for Miss Dorner says that in the country the afternoons are unbearably long and one must have some refreshment as dinner is not served until eight o'clock. If I could only add a little to the afternoons that they find so long! I cannot get everything finished I lay out to do. Good-bye, Martha!" And Cornelli ran off.

CHAPTER IV

THE UNDESIRED OCCURS

ESTHER, the worthy mistress of the kitchen, was in the vegetable garden picking green peas. The warm June sun had ripened them early, and great clusters hung in profusion on the vines.

"Come down here, Cornelli," she called. "Come and see what a lot of peas there are on the vines. Why do you creep around so? Why don't you come all on a run as you always used to do?"

"I am not allowed to do as usual any more," replied Cornelli as she approached. "And now Mina starts in to tell me I must not jump any more—that my hair will get tousled. I just wish I didn't have a single hair on my head, then I could run and jump!"

"No, no, that would make you look dreadful. Just picture yourself! But there is no need to be sad about such a little matter as that," said Esther consolingly. "You just jump around; your hair can always be combed again. Why

76

don't you come into the kitchen any more to see if my baking tastes right?"

"I must not. Miss Dorner has forbidden it. She says it is bad manners," Cornelli informed her.

"Well, well, you might do worse things! But of course you must obey and do as you are told," agreed Esther. "But don't you visit Miss Mina any more when she is preparing the dessert?"

Cornelli shook her head.

Miss Mina had been quick to grasp the fact that a new order of things prevailed in the house and adapted herself to it. When she thought the ladies did not approve the old practices, she dropped them at once and Cornelli had noted her changed attitude.

"It is all the same to me if I must not go into the pantry; I don't care!" Cornelli burst out. "She can eat all that falls off the plate herself! It's all the same to me so long as I can go into the stable to the little kid. It is the most cunning little creature! Have you seen it, Esther?"

"Why, of course I have! Why not?" she responded. "Matthew fetched me out as soon as it was born. Certainly you can pay it visits as long as it is in your own stable. Go out as often as you wish; no one will hinder you."

"Here comes my teacher," called out Cornelli. "Now I must go."

With these words Cornelli ran off to the house, for she had already forgotten that she had been instructed to walk, never to run.

The two ladies sat on the garden bench in the jessamine arbor while Cornelli was occupied with her lessons in the living-room.

"It would be so lovely here, and my cousin would have a really happy life if only that child were a little different," remarked Miss Dorner. "Don't you think, Betty, that she is a most uncouth child?"

"Yes, but careful early training is missing," Miss Grideelen replied, "and perhaps the child has inherited some of her mother's ways."

"Not a single one! You could not picture two people more different than the mother and this child," declared Kitty Dorner. "Cornelia was amiability itself. Always happy, always gay. Always ready to greet everyone with her laughing brown eyes. I would be glad to acknowledge the child resembled the mother in even one tiny trait, for my cousin was so fond of his wife, and, being such an admirable man, surely deserves the pleasure such resemblance would give him."

"It is strange how children do differ from their parents," said Miss Grideelen with regret, "but certainly it will be possible to accomplish something with this child through education. In that way qualities may be cultivated that she does not now possess. It is worth taking pains with her on account of the father."

"I certainly will do so. I am doing it now, as you know, Betty, but so far I can see no results," returned Miss Dorner.

The day was exceedingly hot, and the ladies retired to their rooms immediately after lunch while Cornelli, as was her custom, went to her studies. Then she disappeared. Late in the evening it was still so hot that, as they sat down to dinner, they ordered Miss Mina to throw open all the windows.

"For pity's sake, what has happened to you?" exclaimed Miss Dorner when Cornelli stepped into the room. "We are prostrated with the heat, and here you put on a fur-trimmed dress that you could wear in mid-winter on a sleigh ride! Who in the world suggested such a sense-less thing?"

Cornelli's cheeks were glowing, and little

streams of perspiration trickled down her face from the unbearable heat.

"I have no other dress left," she said.

"Can you understand it?" asked Miss Dorner, appealing to her friend.

"I actually believe this is the fifth dress in which I have seen the child today," Miss Grideelen answered.

"I always have to put on another dress after being in the stable," said Cornelli just a little more stubbornly than before.

"You foolish child!" exclaimed Miss Dorner. "I can well understand why you do not have any fun and are always unhappy. You must be nearly suffocated. Now eat your supper quickly and then go to your room and take off that heavy dress. Certainly you have another. Now these visits to the stable must definitely cease; you must see for yourself what discomfort they bring. If you would only stop screwing your face up into such frowns! You look as if you had two little horns growing out of your forehead, one on each side. There are lots of better amusements than paying visits to the stable. Can you embroider?"

"No!" Cornelli answered abruptly.

"Well, children of your age should be able to do so," said her cousin. "But to teach you how to handle a needle is not just what I came here to do, is it, Betty?"

"It is not at all necessary that Cornelli should learn to embroider just now," rejoined Miss Grideelen. "There are lovely books the child can read; she has shown us a number herself. You must be more fond of reading a good story than of running to the stable; are you not?"

"No, I am not!" returned Cornelli angrily.

"We must pay no attention to her opinions," declared Miss Dorner. "When Cornelli becomes bored she will read her books. You, Miss Mina, must watch Cornelli so that she does not do anything so stupid as to change her clothes five times a day."

When the dinner was over, Cornelli went up to her room and Miss Mina followed her.

"You really must not do such silly things," said the maid as soon as they were on the stairs where her words could not be overheard. "It is just a little too much to watch over you every minute of the day to prevent your changing your dress too often."

"I am not to blame," retorted Cornelli. "She ordered it."

"They will not always smell it when you have been in the stable," continued Miss Mina.

"Oh, but they will!" Cornelli declared. "And if they didn't, I must still obey. They have ordered me to change my dress every time I come from the stable."

"Now, however, the command is that you shall not go into the stable at all," grumbled Mina as she took off the child's thick winter dress. "And now this dress needs cleaning. You give me more trouble than six children properly brought up!"

Miss Mina had never spoken so crossly to Cornelli before for she had always done her best to keep in the child's good graces. But now that did not seem to concern her. Cornelli looked up in mute astonishment, and something gleamed in her eyes that had never been there before. Mina must have understood it, for she said quickly, "I've done nothing to you, and what I am saying is the truth," and with that she left the room.

"If everybody acts like that toward me, I'll act that way too," Cornelli called out enraged, and grabbing the winter dress, she tossed it out

"So that's what you did? Well, another time you will fetch it yourself."

of the window.   After a while Miss Mina came
into the room carrying the dress, and found
Cornelli sitting on the window-sill looking grim-
ly down into the yard.

"Take care the wind does not blow you down
like it did your dress," said Miss Mina a little
unkindly.

"Let it! I don't care!" retorted Cornelli
defiantly.   "And it did not blow the dress down;
I threw it down on purpose."

"So *that's* what you did?   Well, another time
you will fetch it yourself, I promise you that!"
and Miss Mina left the room in anger.

The next morning after lessons were over,
Cornelli was walking across the yard, holding
her teacher's hand and chatting happily.   Her
worries of the day before had been forgotten, for
Mr. Mallinger, her teacher, had been as kind as
ever.   He, at least, had not changed.

"Have you a little rose for me?" he asked
pleasantly as they passed the bushes all in full
bloom.

Cornelli ran from one to another till she had
gathered a lovely nosegay of pink, dark red and
white roses.   As she gave it to the teacher, she
warned him not to prick himself on the thorns,

and then the two parted with a hearty good-bye. Cornelli ran in great leaps and bounds toward the stable. Suddenly she stood stock still. She had just remembered she must not go inside. She could not go and look at the young kid any more and watch its growth. She would not know when the time arrived when she could put a harness on it and take a drive. Perhaps she would not be allowed to do that! But perhaps by that time her father would be home again and everything would be different. She gave a little skip, for the old joyfulness wanted to rise again. She would go to Esther and consult with her as to the whole matter. As she stepped into the house she encountered her cousin coming out of the living-room.

"You have come just at the right time," said the latter. "I want to show you something. Where were you going?"

"Into the kitchen," answered Cornelli.

"There is nothing for you to do in the kitchen. You must not go there. I thought you understood that before meals you were to go upstairs and comb your hair. Do that next, but first come in here so I can tell you something important."

Cornelli followed her cousin into the living-room. Miss Grideelen stood at the window evidently awaiting her friend's return. Miss Dorner led Cornelli over to the sofa and pointed at it.

"You must know who did that," said she. "Now be frank about it."

There were marks of dusty shoe soles on the plush covering, but no imprint of an entire foot, though there could be no doubt someone had walked on the sofa.

"I didn't do it," said Cornelli, her eyes blazing.

"Who in the house, except you, could have done such a thing? Just ask yourself that, Cornelli. It is no question who did it," said Miss Dorner. "Probably it was one of your little jokes, like throwing your dress out of the window. I heard all about that! I wish to tell

you just one thing: this is the last time that you, a girl of ten years, will display such bad manners. As long as I am here, it shall not happen again. You might also spare your good, refined father such a trial too."

"I did not do it! No, I did not do it! No, no!" Cornelli cried out.

"Now, Cornelli, think better of that! Your face is quite red. You see your conscience betrays you," Miss Grideelen interrupted. "It would be much better to say humbly, 'I did it, but I am very sorry and will not do it again!'"

"No, I did not do it! No, no!" screamed Cornelli louder still, and her cheeks glowed with anger and excitement.

"Don't make such a spectacle of yourself," commanded her cousin. "One might think there had been an accident. It is not worth while to waste so many words over it. You should not have made your case worse by denying it; then it all would have been over long ago. You have conducted yourself very badly, and you must not do so again. Now remember!"

"No, I did not do it! I will not say yes, because that is not true!"

"Go to your room, Cornelli," commanded

Miss Dorner, "and smooth out your forehead before you come to table. Your little horns stand straight out when you act that way. You can see for yourself how repulsive you look. Just use your mirror. You deceive yourself if you think there is anyone in the world who will like you when you have those two little black horns on your forehead. Go now, and come back with a different kind of face."

Arriving in her own room, Cornelli's hands grasped at her forehead. Actually, on either side was a protruding point, a firm little projection. Would real horns grow out from them? A dreadful fright seized Cornelli's heart. She thought everybody could see them as they were so easily grasped. Fright, pain, anger, rebellion filled her heart. She could stand it no longer, and she ran out, on her way to the aged Martha.

"No, I did not do it, Martha! I certainly did not do it!" she cried as she burst into the little room. "And when I tell them no, they ought to believe that I did not do it. No, I did not do it! They ought to believe it! I have not told an untruth, for I never did it! But they would not believe me if I said no a hundred times and—"

"Stop a little," counselled old Martha kindly. "Why, you are all out of breath. Come, sit here on your little stool and tell me all about it."

Cornelli could not tell her story calmly, but the very presence of Martha soothed her so that she poured out the tale freely, and she knew she was fully believed. She told about the accusation that had been raised against her, and how, in spite of all her assurances, they insisted she had done it. She was certain they would always believe it, in spite of her denials. At this thought Cornelli grew purple-red with emotion once more, and when she would have broken out again, Martha softly repressed her, putting her hand on her shoulder.

"No, no, Cornelli; just be satisfied that you are in the right. You have been falsely accused and cannot prove it, but the dear Lord knows how it is. He has heard all, and you can be quite calm and happy and look up to Him with a clear conscience and think, 'The good Lord knows it. I have nothing to fear; no reason to be sad.' It would have been quite different if you had done something wicked and had denied it. Then you would have been in dread of the thought that the truth would come to light. You would have been in fear and trembling at the thought, 'There is One who knows that I did it. I cannot hide it from Him.' A false accusation does not always last. There comes a day when the truth is revealed, and even if it is carried into eternity, you will not have to bear it there, for the dear Lord knows how it is."

Cornelli had grown calm with the thought that there was One who knew how it all was, and with the assurance that whenever trouble came again she could say, "Thou knowest, dear God. Thou has seen and heard it all."

"If He would only tell them!" was Cornelli's wish. "The dear God could very well do that and then they would know at once," she said.

"Yes, but that is not the way things happen in this world. We do not know what is best for us as the good Lord does," said Martha quite earnestly, shaking her head. "Don't you see that if we could regulate our affairs, everything would be upside down? We are not able to see an hour ahead, and do not know at any moment what would be good for us, for suddenly something comes up that we do not know about. Then we would give anything at all to undo what yesterday we had forced with all our might. We would make ourselves miserable, and do so over and over again. But if the dear Lord allows something to happen which we do not understand we can rely implicitly on the fact that good will come out of it for us. We have only to wait. When matters press very hard, we always have the consolation of knowing the dear Lord sends what is good for us. But we are forgetting the time, Cornelli. I fear it is already too late for you to reach home in time for your meal."

Under Martha's calming words, Cornelli's dark looks had disappeared, but now deep shadows gathered again over her features.

"Oh, if only I never had to go home again, Martha! And never go to the table! It would be all the same to me even if I had to starve, if I could only stay with you."

"But what are you thinking of, Cornelli? Such a beautiful home as you have! It is not right to think that way about it," Martha said in kindly rebuke. "Just think how many children have no home. How they would thank the dear Lord for one as fine as yours! Now hurry, Cornelli, and be happy that God has given you so much, and bid farewell to the thoughts that grieve you so. Come again soon, and we will be happy together, for there is always something to be happy about."

It seemed to her as long as she was with Martha and listened to her words that there was no reason for grief, but as soon as she entered the home garden and saw the windows of the room where the ladies would already be seated at table, all the trouble that had weighed on her heart rose again within her.

Martha was all wrong; she could not be happy, Cornelli thought to herself. She could not go indoors. She could not eat, anyhow; it seemed to her she could not swallow again, for great stones seemed sticking in her throat. If she could only die from it all! Cornelli thought that would be best, for then everything would be over. She seated herself on the grass behind the thick currant bushes where she could not be seen from the house. In the meanwhile Miss Mina had carried away the last course and was serving the fruit.

"It seems Cornelli thinks little of being a full hour late for meals," remarked Miss Dorner. "Her food is not to be kept warm for her; she must learn to respect time and order."

CORNELLI, HER CHILDHOOD

Mina went out to sit down to her own meal.
Esther had laid the table ready, and she put the
dessert in the cupboard. "The child will have
this when she comes home," she said as she
seated herself. "She has enough to swallow
these days that is not sweet."

"Why can't she get here at the proper time?"
asked Mina angrily. "And she cannot eat all
the dessert, so we might just as well take our
share. There will be enough left,—more than is
good for her health."

"I am not going to serve it," said Esther,
resting her arms firmly on the table as a sign of
her steadfast purpose. "The child must certainly have something to help her swallow all
that happens. She has more to put up with
than ever before in her life. What was it that
went wrong this morning that set up such a row
in the room?"

"Nothing much, that's certain," replied Miss
Mina. "There were a few traces of dust on the
sofa, so they thought Cornelli had stood on it.
The child would not own up to it and the ladies
held to their accusation until the child screamed
like one crazy. All of it was quite unnecessary."

"I am of the opinion, Miss Mina, that you

94

ought to have made an explanation whence the footprints came," said Esther with a sly smile. "When the clock that hangs over the sofa has to be wound, it is quicker to jump up on the sofa than to move that heavy piece of furniture. And when one's boots are laced up early in the morning,"—Esther cast a meaning look down at the neat boots Miss Mina had stretched out under the table—"they are not easily pulled off. Is that not so, Miss Mina?"

"Well, yes; but what about that?" she replied snappishly. "A jump on the sofa would not ruin it, and I have to dust it myself."

"I mean that one could say a word before the ladies accused the child of lying and before Cornelli, angered over the injustice, had started to scream so that it froze the marrow of one's bones."

"Oh, bah! It was not as bad as all that," objected Mina. "Cornelli has long since forgotten all about it. That's the way with children. A heathenish yelling, then out of the door to forget it. Why waste any thought about it?"

"It used to be different," said Esther, smiling. "Then Miss Mina could not do enough for Cornelli. But now all her kindnesses are in another direction. None now for the old house residents."

"Old house residents!" repeated Mina scornfully. "It won't be long before Esther will sing another tune, when the lady of the house gives orders in her kitchen—the lady who is a new resident now."

Esther let her spoon drop. "Good gracious, what are you talking about?" she exclaimed. "Who ever thought of such a thing! Which is intended, the relative or the other?"

"Well, it can't be said exactly," rejoined Mina. "The master of course has not discussed the matter with me; but one must be very dense not to notice what is happening and to understand why the ladies came."

"Good gracious!" said the surprised Esther. "That is a discovery! The cousin is the one, of that you may be sure. She rules the entire house already. But I will say in advance, Miss Mina, I have sung the same tune in this house for the last twelve years and I will continue to sing it, whoever the mistress, you may believe that."

"We shall see," said Mina as she rose to see

if either of the ladies needed anything further.

Cornelli awoke out of a sound sleep. At first she did not know where she was. She lay on the grass behind the currant bushes. Then she remembered that she had dropped down there as she came from Martha's at midday, and how tired and sleepy she had grown. She must have fallen asleep. It was evening now, for no sunshine lay on the garden, though the sky was still bright in spite of approaching twilight. A longing such as she had never known before seized Cornelli.

She felt a desire to nibble at everything round about her—bushes and branches, leaves and flowers and, above all, the unripe plums on the tree above her. If she only had a piece of bread! Cornelli sprang to her feet and ran to the house.

"Lively, lively!" called Esther to her through the open kitchen window. "They have just sat down to the table; you have come just in the nick of time."

Cornelli rushed to her room, snatched a thick scarf from among her belongings and wound it around her head, then ran into the dining-room and sat down hastily at her place.

"Well, are you back?" asked Miss Dorner. "A well-bred child would at least say good-evening when she enters the room after a long absence."

"Good-evening," said Cornelli, and then finished her soup in unusual haste.

"Where do you come from after all this time?" asked her cousin.

"From the garden," was the answer.

"That may well be, but where were you before?" Miss Dorner inquired.

"With Martha," replied Cornelli.

"If you could only learn to give your answers more agreeably," remarked the cousin, "it would be to your own advantage. There is nothing very attractive about you, and you might become more winning if you had that grace. You should really strive to improve your ways. If you wish to visit this woman again and remain for any length of time, you must first ask my permission. You must not stay away so long again. Your absence today deserves punishment, but I will not say anything more about it this time. Why look so sorrowful? Have you a toothache?"

"No," was Cornelli's curt answer.

"Have you a headache?"

"No."

"What is the matter with you then?"

"Nothing."

"Cornelli, you must not resort to such subterfuges when there is nothing the matter," reproved Miss Dorner. "Why wind a scarf around your head like a gypsy? Don't ever come to the table that way! Betsy, did you ever see anything like it? Can you understand how a rational child can act so?"

The next morning when Cornelli went to breakfast, she wore no scarf around her head, but nevertheless was a strange sight to see.

"You look for all the world like a New Zealander," said Miss Dorner. "Do you think you improve your appearance by drawing your hair down over your face?"

"No," said Cornelli fiercely.

"Nor I, either," said Miss Dorner. "I cannot comprehend you. What will you pull down over your forehead, I wonder, if your hair is brushed back?"

"My fur cap," answered Cornelli, truthfully.

"Such caprices!" exclaimed Miss Dorner. "I believe the child is quite capable of pulling a fur cap over her head when the thermometer stands at eighty, and wearing it right down to her nose if once she gets that into her head. I have never seen such a child! I don't know what to do with her!"

As a matter of fact, Cornelli looked as though she had never seen how European girls combed their hair. She had drawn her thick dark locks down over her forehead in long, uneven strands until it hung in her eyes, and she had glued it firmly to her skin. Her purpose seemed to be to keep it in place, just as she wished it.

"You look hideous, Cornelli! No one will want to see you when you go around looking like that. This caprice may be turned to your advantage, otherwise nothing can be done for you," and with these words Miss Dorner rose and left the room, Miss Grideelen following her.

In the evening the following letter went to Mr. Hellmut:

"Illerbach, June 20th.

Dear Cousin:—

Everything here is going well; you have an exceptionally capable manager for your business. And in the house, in the garden, and in the stables the best of order prevails, as I see it, and as far as I can learn from those of the servants I feel to be thoroughly reliable. You have a lovely estate, rich in fruit and flowers and vegetables. I never thought it would be like this when I wandered over the estate years ago with my friend Cornelia.

But now I come to the principal news, which unfortunately is not gratifying. I cannot understand where your daughter inherited such a disposition. She shows none of your open ways, nor any of the happy, sociable traits of your wife Cornelia. The child has a sullen, unpleasant disposition, her manners are common and repulsive, and added to this is an unheard-of obstinacy. Words have no effect on her. Chastisement and discipline I must leave to you. I will leave nothing undone so far as good example and words of warning go as long as I am here, and my friend will aid me. But I can not encourage you in the hope that the child will ever bring you much happiness. Such an obstinate nature will grow more refractory every year. I hope the successful outcome of your business undertakings will bring you the satisfaction which your home life does not offer, but which you so richly deserve.

> Your devoted cousin,
> KITTY DORNER."

CHAPTER V

A NEW ARRIVAL AT ILLERBACH

OLD Matthew was tidying the gravel path in the garden as Cornelli stepped out of the house and came slowly along. She had a book in her hand and seated herself on the bench under the hazelnut tree. Holding the book in her lap, she looked on while Matthew smoothed the path. "Come along with me, Cornelli," he said, looking up. "You have not been in the stable for a long while. You ought to see how the little kid has grown!"

Cornelli shook her head, her only answer, and though Matthew looked toward her several times, he said no more.

Now Esther came by with a great basket, bound for the vegetable garden. "You must have a specially lovely book," she called to the child, "otherwise you would not sit so still. I know you."

Cornelli shook her head.

"No?" laughed Esther. "Then come along with me and I'll show you what a quantity of yellow plums there are this year. The tree is loaded, and the fruit is already yellowing."

"I don't care," responded Cornelli.

"No? Well, and such plums!" exclaimed Esther. "The pears are beginning to ripen too. Won't you come and see how long it will be until they are good eating?"

"No," came Cornelli's refusal.

Esther went her way, and Matthew shortly afterward joined her. "What is the matter with the child, Esther?" he asked. "She has changed entirely. One would not recognize our former gay Cornelli. And why does she have her hair hanging down over her face? She is not our old Cornelli, either in appearance or manners."

"That's exactly what I say!" declared Esther. "I do not know what is the matter. One scarcely sees the child any more, and when you do meet her anywhere, she does not have a word to say. We never hear her singing and laughing any more, and her face is so sorrowful all the time that it is painful to see. How happy the child used to be! But they say she must be educated. It may be so, but since she is getting an education, she is much changed, and not for the better.

But perhaps things will be better when her education is finished."

"It's a mother she needs," said Matthew. "It is pretty hard for a child to grow up without a mother, for she is missed at every step. How easy it is when a child can take everything to its mother, its pleasures and its pains."

"One would think you still run to your mother with everything that happens to you," said Esther a little ironically.

"I would like to well enough," Matthew assured her. "I know what my mother was to me, and I pity every child that has none, even if it has everything else in the world."

Matthew went off, but he turned a pitying look toward the bench where Cornelli still sat quite motionless, the book having slipped to the ground.

Shortly afterward Mr. Mallinger stepped into the garden and walked toward the house, and when Cornelli saw him she went to meet him.

"I could not get here today at nine o'clock," he explained, "but I think one hour is better than none. Therefore here I am at eleven. I hope you have spent the two morning hours pleasantly and profitably."

"No, I haven't," said Cornelli drily.

"But you have a splendid book in your hand. What is it all about?"

"I don't know," answered Cornelli.

"Well, come, let us get to our studies. Your reading has not made a specially deep impression, I see. Let us hope our lesson hour will do better."

After they had entered the house and seated themselves in their places, the teacher said, "It appears to me, Cornelli, that your hair is in your way. Can't you arrange it better?"

"No, that cannot be done, never, never!" said Cornelli with violent emotion, and she pressed her hair firmly to her forehead.

"Well, well, that is not my affair," said the teacher soothingly. "Only it looks to me like a rather disfiguring style of wearing it. I should think you would feel better without these weeping-willow drapings over your eyes."

Cornelli still held both hands pressed firmly to her forehead, as though the teacher might try by force to put her hair in order. But he passed on to the lessons quite peacefully.

When the ladies were leaving the lunch table, Miss Dorner said: "Now no more running away at once, Cornelli. You really must begin to lead an orderly life! When you are through with your lessons you must read some good book; you have a number. You have plenty of time for rambles and paying visits after the evening coffee."

The lesson preparations were, as usual, quickly finished. Then Cornelli took her book and seated herself on the garden bench as she had done in the morning, laying the book in her lap till it fell to the ground. She gazed around at the trees and at the ground, but she really did not see anything at all. At the coffee hour, she seated herself punctually at the table, quickly swallowed what was poured out for her as though it were medicine that had to be taken. Then she sat motionless, her eyebrows drawn together in a frown for she had to remain at table until the ladies arose, as Miss Dorner insisted she observe this good habit.

"Don't make such horns! One can see them even through your hanging hair, you draw your forehead together so. It won't be long now before you may leave the table."

At last the ladies arose to go into the garden. Cornelli crept along behind them, then turned unexpectedly around the corner of the house and made directly across the meadow to the path.

"To sit under the hazel tree with a good book to read is a pleasure that does not come to many children," said Miss Dorner, seating herself on the bench. "For this reason alone you ought to wear a happy face and to be thankful instead of frowning and pouting, Cornelli—Well, where has she gone again?" she broke off, as she looked around.

"She disappeared as soon as we stepped out of doors," answered Miss Grideelen. "Cornelli is certainly a peculiar child!"

"I am only too sorry on her father's account, for he longs for a happy household," continued Miss Dorner. "It will never be his with this daughter who daily becomes more headstrong and cross. Everyone in the house feels this, so Mina tells me, and I am wondering just how disagreeable she will make things for the household in two or three years from now. Oh, my poor cousin! What does his lovely estate avail him?"

"You know, Kitty, that many things can happen in two years that may change the entire household and that now are quite unforeseen,"

Miss Grideelen consoled her, "and let us hope that such will be the case for the benefit of your cousin."

For Cornelli there were no more carefree leapings and skippings. She crept along the edge of the path looking down at the ground and did not even look up to see the birds that were singing so gayly in the trees. Away to the right and left stretched the meadow, and though it was abloom with red daisies and blue forget-me-nots, flowers Cornelli loved above all others, she did not even glance at them.

Martha saw the child approaching and came out. She looked worried as she asked tenderly, "What is the matter, Cornelli? Can you not be happy again?"

"No, I never can be so again," answered Cornelli as she entered the little cottage and seated herself on the little stool that Martha had placed ready for her. Cornelli did not speak quickly and angrily as she had done before but with a deep sigh she added, "Oh, if I had only never learned to read!"

"What? Why, child, that is absurd! You should learn what it means to wish to read something and not be able to and then starting over and over again without being able to get it clear. That is just what happened to me today and if you could not help me, then I should never be able to understand it. Those who can read and write easily are very fortunate and I often wish I were able to do it as well as my little Cornelli. And you have such lovely books that your father gave to you,—don't you like them, Cornelli?"

"Yes, they are pretty but dull, Martha," answered Cornelli. "There is nothing in them except tales, descriptions of great men and discoveries. Papa said he enjoyed them very much when he was young, but I guess he was different. Now I may not run around and roam through the woods or go into the stable, when that is what I love to do; but must just sit and read a dull book. Oh, I wish no one had ever written a book; then we would not have to read them."

"Well, you see, Cornelli, that would not suit everyone," answered Martha. "But come now and help me to read the letter I received today."

Cornelli was very glad to assist her dear friend and taking the letter, asked, "Who wrote it?"

"That is just what I cannot decipher," said

Martha. "I only know it came from the city."

Cornelli read the letter aloud. It asked if the room was still unoccupied and if Mrs. Wolf could accommodate a twelve-year-old boy for several weeks. There was no need of special care as he was not sick, but failing in health somewhat. Fresh air and good milk every day were the chief needs and if no word came to the contrary, the boy would arrive the middle of July. The letter was signed "Nika Halm, rector's widow."

"Oh, how easily you read!" said Martha in wonder when Cornelli had finished. "I could never have figured it out. Just think, a rector's wife will bring her son to my house. That is something to be proud of. Surely I will give him the best of care and attention. I must ask Matthew if he can give me fresh milk every morning and evening. The only pity is that a little girl is not coming, for then you would have a playmate. However, you can play together. Are you not just a little pleased?"

"No, not even a little bit," replied Cornelli abruptly. "I know he will not wish to have anything to do with me, and I know why. It is all the same to me whether a boy or girl comes.

I do not want to have anything to do with him."

"You did not use to be like that, Cornelli. You were friendly and merry with everyone. What has come over you?" asked Martha, a little worried. "You no longer look around with bright eyes, and I think your hair falls down a little too low. May I not smooth it back a little?"

Martha brought a comb and started to use it, but Cornelli objected. "No, let it alone, Martha! It must be so! It must stay that way as long as I live."

"Oh, I do not believe that. It is a pity to wear it so. Why, half your face is hidden, and one would scarcely know you," said Martha regretfully. "What do the ladies say about it?"

"Miss Dorner is angry with me and she says I am the most obstinate creature in the world; that nobody can train me," Cornelli reported truthfully, "and that no child is so hideous as I am. She declares no one will ever like me and I know that is true," she added.

"But I think, Cornelli, that you should do as the ladies wish. That would be right," was Martha's opinion, "and you would like them, and other people would like you too."

"No, no! You do not know what is the trouble, Martha," said Cornelli anxiously. "I will do everything else they tell me, but I cannot comb my hair back. For then it would be much worse, and people could see it."

Martha shook her head.

"I do not know what you mean, but come to me as often as ever you can, Cornelli. No matter who is with me, I shall always love you most; and it would cause me pain if you did not continue coming. I would sooner have no one in my room, although it will give me great pleasure to have the rector's son stay with me."

"Well, I will come again, Martha," promised Cornelli. "We can stay in your kitchen by ourselves; I want to be alone with you. I cannot come on Monday, when they arrive; but I will on Tuesday. You will please come out into the kitchen, Martha."

This Martha promised to do and Cornelli started back to her home the way she had come, but not once did she turn aside to pick the blue forget-me-nots that brightened the meadow.

When Monday arrived Cornelli was just a little curious to know whether a carriage would drive up to Martha's little house in which a proud city lady with a high feather hat would be sitting who would gaze down disdainfully on her. Cornelli took up a position at the garden hedge, where she could look down the road. No carriage came, either in the morning or in the afternoon; of that she was sure for she watched continually. That suited Cornelli exactly. The next day, as soon as the hour arrived when she was permitted to leave, she wandered over to Martha's house.

"I am glad they have not come, so I can be alone with you and we need not go into the kitchen—"

Thus spoke Cornelli on entering, then suddenly stood stock still, for at the table sat a strange boy, while Martha was busy clearing away the supper things. He had come after all, and he had heard her say she was happy not to have found him there. Seeing that Cornelli quickly turned to withdraw, the lad burst out laughing and called to her, "No, no! Please step inside, for we should become acquainted. Mrs. Martha has already told me about you. Please come in!" he continued as he saw Cornelli hesitate to enter. "If you prefer to be alone with her, I can go up to my room."

Cornelli felt that it was very nice of him not to be angry at her words and to wish to make room for her, so she stepped in. Martha had already placed her stool for her and now greeted her with the usual show of affection.

"I have been expecting you, Cornelli. Come, sit down a little while with our guest. His name is Dino Halm, and I have told him yours.

You will certainly have a nice time together. I have to go upstairs for awhile, and if you need anything, Cornelli, you will find me in the little room."

Martha knew that the acquaintance would progress better if the two were left alone and, besides, she could use the time in unpacking the newcomer's things and arranging them in his cupboard and drawers.

"What made you think we had not come?" asked Dino as Martha left the room and Cornelli sat silent before him.

"Because I did not see the carriage."

"The carriage? Well, I can believe that," said Dino. "We had more than an hour's walk, nearly two, from the railroad station to this house. Do you always ride in a carriage when you want to go to the station?"

"Yes. I ride with papa," answered Cornelli.

"Where do the horses always come from?"

"Out of the stable," was the reply.

"Do you have your own stable and two horses, just to drive out?" asked Dino in great astonishment.

"Yes, we have two brown ones and six others that haul the iron from the foundry over there."

"Mercy me, you have eight horses!" exclaimed Dino. "You are a lucky girl to be able to sit in a carriage and be driven around!"

"Can't you do that too?" asked Cornelli.

"No, surely not; never in my life!" replied Dino conclusively. "In the first place I have no father any more, and in the second place, we have no stable, much less any horses. How lucky you are! Have you anything else in your stable?"

"Well, not much. Only six cows and a big gray stable cat," Cornelli informed him. "And an old goat with a young snow-white kid. I've tied a red ribbon on the kid's neck. You are to drink milk that is furnished by our cows."

"Oh, I'll be very glad to do that!" declared Dino. "May I go into your stable and have a look at the horses?"

"Why, yes; Matthew will gladly show them to you, and Martha will let you go, I know. If I could only go with you!" and she breathed a deep sigh.

"You can do that all right if the stable belongs to you. Who is there to hinder you?" said Dino with assurance. "Do you know what we could do? We will hitch the kid to a little cart.

Won't it make a smart outfit? The kid can pull you along and I'll be the coachman. I saw a little carriage like that once on our city promenade."

Cornelli had harbored this plan, but she was not allowed to go to the stable, and now she knew she could not run around and be happy as formerly. She made no reply, but only gave a long sigh, deeper than the last, as she realized this was the chief reason she was not her old merry self.

"What makes you sigh as though you had to bear the weight of a mountain, and could hardly carry the load?" asked Dino.

"That I can't tell to anyone. You would too if you had the worry I have," replied Cornelli.

"There is nothing in the world I could not tell," asserted Dino. "There is always one's mother, and when you tell her, everything comes right again. Just go along and tell her about it, and then all will be easy and everything right again."

"Well, now I can say to you what you said to me. You are a lucky person, much more lucky than I," said Cornelli with emotion. "I cannot go to my mother, because I have none. Now

117

you understand what a good time I have! You would not change places with me now, would you?"

"I did not know that you had no mother," he said in quick sympathy, for he pictured his mother in his mind's eye, how she looked at him with overflowing love and made him light of heart when anything weighed on him. Cornelli had to miss all that!

The stable, the horses and the great garden with the abundance of fruit about which Martha had already told him took on a different light, and he said decidedly, "No, I would not change with you." But a deep sympathy for the motherless girl rose in Dino's heart, though he tried to hide it a little. Now he could understand why Cornelli looked so peculiar that her appearance had struck him immediately as she entered. There was no mother to arrange hair and dress as it should be.

"Look here, Cornelli," he began again, "let us be friends! First of all I advise you to brush the hair off your forehead; now one cannot see your eyes. No one does their hair like that. What do you do to it to make it stay pasted down so tightly on your forehead?"

"I glue it," explained Cornelli.

"Horrible! Come, let me cut off the sticky mass. Then your forehead and eyes will be free. This way you can hardly see."

Dino had seized a pair of shears that lay in Martha's work-basket but Cornelli repulsed him with both hands and screamed aloud, "Leave it alone! It must stay so! Take away the scissors!"

"I don't want to hurt you; don't scream so," said Dino calmly as he put back the scissors. "On the contrary, I want to do you a kindness. If my sisters Nika and Agnes saw you, they would laugh at you. They would not like the way you paste down your hair at all."

"I'm well aware of that, but they do not need to see me," said Cornelli petulantly. "No one needs to see me. I know that no one likes me, but it's all the same to me," and with that Cornelli ran off.

Dino gazed in great astonishment at the door through which the little girl had disappeared so unceremoniously, and when Martha stepped into the room and looked surprised to find Cornelli's forsaken stool, he said, "My, that is a queer child! I did not think she could be so unsociable." And he related how they had been talking when all of a sudden she had run off without saying good-bye. He surely did not mean to offend her.

Martha shook her head as she said, "Cornelli was not always like that. I am worried about her. She has changed so much. You must not think she is queer or that she always runs away in a sudden fit of temper, for it is not true. This is something new. Oh, if I could only hear my Cornelli laugh and sing as she used to do! I hoped that with a good comrade like you, her old happiness would return. Perhaps it will, for this is only the first day of your acquaintance."

"Cornelli certainly will never come to see me again," declared Dino much confused. "She ran off so vexed and angered."

But even though Cornelli had declared she knew no one cared for her and that it made no difference to her, that could hardly have been the truth, for when she reached home she crept up to her room, seated herself on a footstool and, bowing her head in both hands, wept bitterly.

CHAPTER VI

A NEW FRIEND

FOR a number of days Cornelli did not go to Martha's cottage and her absence grieved the little old lady for several reasons. First, she loved the child as though she were her own, and she sadly missed the daily visits. Next, she knew something out of the ordinary must have occurred to keep Cornelli away, for ever since she was a very little child, never a day passed without her running in to tell old Martha all that had happened to her. Then, too, she was sorry Cornelli remained away on account of her guest. She had told Dino so much about her, how merry and amusing she was, and how he would find her a splendid playmate, and now nothing came of it; Cornelli stayed away.

During these days Martha could not do enough to make her lodger comfortable, and a close friendship sprang up between the two. After Dino had taken his daily walk and done his lessons, he sat down beside Martha to listen to the many interesting tales she had to tell.

Most of all she spoke about Mr. Hellmut and his wife. Martha had known her as a little child. Then she would soon begin about Cornelli. Such a happy, merry, amusing child she had never known, she declared again and again. Dino insisted he could not understand that and when Martha said she was the loveliest child she had ever seen, he burst out laughing.

"Why, she looks exactly like a little owl! One cannot even see her eyes. However, I wish she would come again," he added, for he really wished to discover if Cornelli could be the merry little girl Martha believed her.

That evening after Dino had gone to his little room, old Martha quickly tied on one of her best aprons, took her big shawl out of the wardrobe, and throwing it over her shoulders, stepped softly out of the house and took her way toward Mr. Hellmut's. There was a bright light at the kitchen window as well as in the one looking out on the garden. Martha entered the kitchen, and found Esther and Miss Mina at the supper table.

"Do sit down, Martha! You must have earned a rest. How are you?" she asked while she pushed three dishes and a bottle over to her guest. "Take them; do take them! There is ever so much left, and I shall be glad to cook something fresh tomorrow."

"Many thanks, Esther; I have had my supper," rejoined Martha. "But it is very kind of you to wish me to join you and I thank you just the same."

"No thank-you for me! Anyone can eat what I have cooked, even the Czar of Russia himself, and you are not quite *that* grand," insisted Esther while she heaped the plate with a juicy cut of the roast, macaroni, and stewed plums.

Martha found herself unable to reject Esther's invitation, so she began her second supper which was much more sumptuous than her first.

"What's happened, Martha, that you come so late?" Esther now asked, curious to know the meaning of a visit from Martha at so unusual an hour.

"I wanted to ask you something, Esther, and I thought I would disturb your work less in the evening," explained Martha. "Cornelli has not been over to see me the entire week, and you know she always comes every day. I thought that perhaps the ladies do not wish her to visit such a humble old woman. I could understand that very well. Do you think that is what keeps her away?"

"No, I do not believe anything of the kind," replied Esther. "They know from Miss Mina that our master likes you. But you have no idea how the child has changed in all her ways. One hardly knows her. Who used to come running into the kitchen three or four times a day? Who used to sing and flit about the garden like a bird morning, evening, all day long? Who picked the delicious berries, the yellow plums and the juicy red cherries over there on the young trees, so that it was a joy to see? Cornelli, always Cornelli! And now? None of it! The berries have dried on the bushes long since and the fine sour cherries spoiled on the trees. The golden plums—such lovely little plums!—lie by the dozen beneath the tree. They are meant for children. Of course the ladies do not want them and they cannot be cooked, so they fall and lie there, and Cornelli passes by without raising her head."

Martha was too modest to say how gladly she would carry a little basket of the lovely plums to her young lodger, she had no fruit at all for him,

124

and how delicious he would think them. But he was staying with her, and it would look as though she were asking for herself and she could not do that.

"Well, Esther," she said, "I certainly have noticed that Cornelli has changed, but, God willing, matters will improve. The child will become accustomed to the new life, and it will be a good thing for her to have someone bring her up properly."

Esther shrugged her shoulders significantly but said nothing.

"Is the child in her room yonder, or has she gone out? I want to tell her to come to see me again, as you say the ladies have no objection."

Esther was saved a reply for at that moment Cornelli crept along the passage, and when she caught sight of Martha, her face lighted up with joy and she ran quickly to greet her.

"I came to find out if you were sick, or if anything stood in the way of your visiting me any more," said Martha, taking Cornelli's hand in a hearty fashion. "It seems such a long time since you have been to see me, child."

"It has been long to me too," said Cornelli in a voice that trembled.

"Then come soon again—tomorrow, and every day, as you used to do," Martha begged.

"No, I am not coming," rejoined Cornelli.

"Why not, Cornelli?"

"Because the boy is there. He can't bear me, and I can't bear him either," asserted Cornelli.

Martha energetically declared this was a mistaken notion, and told how, on the contrary, Dino asked daily after Cornelli and would be so pleased if she would come again. He had no playmate, and to pass day after day alone was tedious for him. It was certainly not his fault that Cornelli did not like him, and he did not dislike her or he would not desire her return. "Tell me, Cornelli, why you do not like Dino?" Martha finally asked.

"I will come again tomorrow," Cornelli said, and that satisfied Martha. Much pleased, she bade Cornelli good-bye.

The next day Cornelli arrived at Martha's at her usual hour, and found her friend waiting for her among her carnations on the little porch.

"Dino is so pleased that you are coming, Cornelli," said Martha, stretching out her hand in welcome. "He has just come home from drinking milk. See, there he comes!"

126

CORNELLI, HER CHILDHOOD

Dino had heard her, and now opened the door and stepped outside. "Why did you stay away so long?" he asked, putting out his hand.

Cornelli did not reply, but both stepped into the room and seated themselves at the table, just as on the first day they met.

"Your little kid grows more cunning every day," said Dino. "It is still wearing your red bow and frisks about so happily. You should see it!"

"I don't care if I never see it again," responded Cornelli ungraciously.

"Now that is not true," said Dino, laughing pleasantly. "When one speaks the way you do and uses that tone, one is not actually indifferent about a matter. One is only feeling bitter. I know that right well, for I do the same thing."

Cornelli was so surprised at Dino's keen perception that she stared at him in silence.

"Yes, I know quite well how it is," he repeated. "But you have no reason to feel bitter. Yours is the loveliest kind of a life. That is what I think every morning and evening when I go to your stable for milk and look over into the garden and see all that fine fruit, the trees heavy with golden plums, and the bushes bend-

9   127

ing under their load of berries. And then the two lovely horses in their separate stalls in your stable! Matthew tells me your father drives out with you every week, and that you can have everything in the garden because you are the only child in the house."

"If there were only twelve or twenty children in the house, it would be quite different!" Cornelli burst out with passion. "But I am all alone and cannot speak a word to anybody. And when one is hated and despised by everybody, and things get worse and worse—oh, you do not know how it is! I only wish I could die!" and Cornelli suddenly put her head down on the table and gave way to a torrent of tears.

Dino looked quite alarmed; he had had no wish to make her sad, and he did not understand her words. But he did know that she had no mother, and that in itself was so sad that he could understand Cornelli's tears. She might well cry, especially as she was an only child. This thought filled him with such keen sympathy for her that he said in the gentlest of tones, "Come, Cornelli! It is indeed sad you have no mother but you must not think that you are entirely alone and that nobody wishes to help you. Look here! I will be your friend and help you, but you must tell me quite frankly what troubles you so. I do not know, and I did not understand what you said. You must tell me all the facts."

"I can't do that; I can't tell anybody!" sobbed out Cornelli.

"Yes, yes, you can. Come now, don't cry any more but tell me everything. Then I can surely help you. I'll find a way. Come, please tell me!" Dino took Cornelli's hands and drew them gently away from her face.

"No, no, I can't!" she declared in distress.

"Oh, but you can! First we'll push the hair aside; it is sticking to your forehead, and it's in your eyes, too. You cannot see with it like that." And Dino pushed the low hanging, sticky hair back as far as he could.

"Now you can see it! Now you've already seen what it is and will make a commotion about it," cried Cornelli in despair.

"I do not see anything except that you look a thousand times better than with your thick hair hanging in your face," declared Dino.

"No, no! I know very well how it is!" exclaimed Cornelli and she tried to draw the hair down again. "You will not admit it because you want to be my friend. But I know about it and everybody sees it and hates me."

"What *are* you crying about?" asked Dino. "I certainly do not know what you mean. You are imagining something. People often do that."

"No, I am not, and there are people who can see it, I know that quite well. You must not believe I am inventing something. Otherwise I would have no such fear as I have. It keeps me awake ever so long each night, and it is growing worse and worse. Soon it cannot be hidden any more, and then there will not be a single person who will not hate me. You will too; I know it very well."

"I swear to you here and now that I will never hate you, whatever happens."

Still Cornelli hesitated. "Will you be my friend even if no one else is? Even if things are quite different?" she urged.

"Yes, I promise, and here's my hand on it!" exclaimed Dino, and he followed up his words with a hearty shake of the hand. "Now you can see how it is, for no one ever goes back on a promise when he has given his hand over it.

You can be absolutely sure I will remain your friend forever."

Joy overspread Cornelli's face. Now she had a friend for all time, come what might!

"I'll tell you what it is," she offered, "but you must promise you will tell no one in the world, as long as you live."

Dino promised with another handshake.

"Just look here," now said Cornelli somewhat timidly as she pushed the strands of hair off her face. "Here on either side of my forehead I have a great bump. They keep on growing and growing, and every time I make a surly face and draw my forehead into a frown, they grow faster than ever. But I have to frown for I can never be happy any more and can never, never laugh again. So the bumps grow bigger every day. At last they will be like horns. All I can do is to hide them, but at last they will stick out through my hair and I will be unable to cover them. Then everyone will see them and despise me, and all the children will wish to throw stones at me. Oh, oh!" and Cornelli again put her head down on her arms and groaned in her distress.

Dino had listened to all this in astonishment, for he had never heard anything like it.

"But, Cornelli, why do you wrinkle your forehead up in a frown if the bumps grow quicker when you do? It would be much better if you had only merry thoughts and laughed all the time. Then you would have a happy face and perhaps the bumps would go away."

"I can't! I can't any more," lamented Cornelli. "I know I make horrid faces and am so hideous that no one likes to look at me. Just because I know people think I am hideous, I make an ugly face when anyone looks at me. It is impossible for me to be happy and to laugh because I am always thinking that the frightful things on my forehead will grow bigger. I can do nothing—not a thing! You have no idea how it is! And as long as I live I must be like that, with everybody against me. I am sure you could not laugh if you were like that."

"But you should try to think of something quite different. Then you would forget the whole affair and life would not look so dreary. Just forget about it; then your trouble will grow less for certain. If you keep thinking of it all the time, you will naturally believe it grows bigger," said Dino, who gave sound advice though he did not quite fathom her difficulty. "Come, I will tell you a little story and that will set you to thinking of something else. Once upon a time there was an old copper kettle— there, you see you have started to laugh already!"

"Yes, that will be a lovely story—about an old copper kettle!" exclaimed Cornelli.

"Why, certainly it *is* a lovely story. Just listen to a little more. The copper kettle had a step-brother who was a wash-boiler—now you have laughed again, you see! That's the way! They went to Paris together, and there was a revolution there."

"What is a revolution?" eagerly.

"You see the story really interests you," said Dino greatly pleased, "and you have hardly any wrinkles on your forehead because you are giving attention to something else. Did I not guess well what you must do? Now I'll continue. A revolution is when no one will stay in his place, the place where he belongs, and everything gets unglued.

"Unglued?" interrupted Cornelli. "Why, glue is used to hold the legs of chairs firm when they get rickety."

"Just so!" agreed Dino. "You see when all law and order begins to get rickety, like the chairs when the glue falls out, everything crashes and tumbles down. They say everything has come unglued. Do you understand?"

"Yes. But how does the story go?"

"That pleased these travelers very well," continued Dino, "for they were filled with discontent. The copper kettle had thought for a long time it would rather be something else, and not always be boiling fats and wearing rust underneath; it wanted to be something better. The wash-boiler had similar thoughts. It was sure it would make as good a tea-kettle as any other. And then it would stand on the master's table instead of out in the wash-house. So the two kettles joined the revolution. They were both good talkers, and gained fame through making many public speeches. The wash-boiler had learned how from the laundresses and the copper kettle from the cooks. So they were asked what high places they desired. The copper kettle wanted to be an ice-chest, with fine shining wood outside, and filled inside with glistening ice. The wash-boiler longed to be a tea-kettle, and stand on the master's table. Both became just what they wanted to be. But the copper kettle had always been used to a comfortable fire, and when it was filled with ice it began to shake with a chill, and its teeth chattered as it gazed around trying to find a bit of fire. But not an ember was near. Added to the cold, it suffered intolerable hunger, for it had always been used to having the fattest morsels that were cooked in it. Now it could swallow only lumps of ice, nothing more. The fact that it glistened all over gave it no pleasure for it could only think:

'Freezing and starvation are frightful!'

"In the meantime the tea-kettle stood on the master's beautifully appointed table. Many young and beautifully dressed ladies sat around the table, eating off plates bordered with gold and drinking out of cups of delicate china. This flattered the tea-kettle and it said to itself: 'Now I can rival them all!' Then one of the ladies said: 'I smell laundry soap; I think it comes from the tea-kettle. What does that mean?' Her neighbor laughed and said, 'I have noticed that a long time. I can only hope it has not been used for washing stockings.' Then they all gazed at the tea-kettle, smelled it and turned up their noses in disgust. The tea-kettle lost its assurance, for well did it remember how many hundreds of stockings had been boiled in it. Until this moment it had had no suspicion that the laundry soap would cling to it in its new form. It grew quite frightened and anxious, and could only think how it could run away and return to the place where it was held in honor; for it had been a good, sound wash-boiler.

"Suddenly the revolution ended. Then said the lady of the house in which the ice-chest stood, 'This wretched ice-chest which the revolution forced on me in place of my good old closet must go. Every piece of ice that comes out of it smells of onion soup.' That was the soup that the copper kettle had always cooked especially well. 'Lulu, throw it out with the junk.' Then Lulu, the manservant, and Lala, the housemaid, lifted the ice-chest and with a great toss threw it out on a large heap of old iron, bones and sweepings in the back yard. It was such a powerful throw that every part of the ice-chest cracked. Now, when the copper kettle felt all its members falling to pieces and knew it must meet a sad end, it said with a groan, 'Oh, if I had only kept out of the revolution! If I were only home over my comfortable coal fire! Oh, if I never—' And just then it fell to pieces.

"On the same day the young lady on whose table the tea-kettle stood said, 'Now I've had enough of this wash-soap boiler. I will have a natural-born tea-kettle, not an imitation. Away with it!' The servant caught up the kettle and dashed it out on the refuse heap in the back yard. It happened to be the same rubbish heap on which its relative had been thrown, and in its fall it broke its own and also its step-brother's last whole bones. In its agonies it shrieked out,

'Oh, if I had only kept out of the revolution! Oh, if I were only in my peaceful home in the steaming wash-house!' Then it was squeezed flat by the old revolution rifles that were tossed out on top of it. And that ends the story."

"Yes, they were right. If they had only stayed out of the revolution!" exclaimed Cornelli in sympathy.

"Yes, and I was also right," declared Dino in triumph. "You see how it has helped you to think of something else. You have not so much as a single wrinkle on your forehead and you have brushed aside your hair. You look like another girl—I scarcely know you."

In fact, Cornelli had been so eager not to lose a word of the story that she had pushed all her low-hanging hair to one side, because it annoyed her, and forgetting why her locks must hang down, she had swept them all off her forehead, and her face had glowed with interest.

"Come, see for yourself," demanded Dino of her as he took a small mirror from the wall and held it in front of Cornelli.

"No, I don't want to see," she cried out, and swiftly drew her hair down into her eyes, and knitted her forehead into a frown.

"Don't do like that," remonstrated Dino, hanging the mirror up again. "Now I know a way to help you, I will do it every day. You must promise to come, and you will soon see how you can forget all that so distresses you, and in the end you will be quite merry again."

Cornelli shook her head, and said, "No, I don't believe that. You can't do anything to prevent it from getting worse," and she pulled a little more hair down into her face. However, she shook hands with Dino and she promised to come again, for this visit had been very pleasant.

After that Cornelli went to Martha's cottage daily, and the good woman rejoiced to hear Cornelli's laughter ring out once more, for she had grieved over the change that had come to this joyful little girl. She liked best to leave the children alone together, for then it seemed they were gayest. Their hearty laughter would peal out now and again, and she prayed that nothing would happen to interrupt their happy intercourse. Now Cornelli listened to the stories Dino told with such intense fervor that one would think she herself were one of the characters, and in her eagerness her hair was swept aside, her eyes sparkled and a laughing face gazed up at the storyteller as she lost herself in the tale. But let anything be mentioned that reminded Cornelli of her own life and the sunshine would suddenly leave her face, the forehead pucker into a frown and the long strands of hair hide the eyes.

Martha counted on these daily meetings doing much for Cornelli; she was sure the happy comrade on whose sunny brow no wrinkle ever appeared could banish the shadows from Cornelli's face.

However, as soon as Cornelli left the little

cottage and reached her own garden, her sorrowful self returned, and Martha, who always gazed after the departing child, could see that once again the strands of hair disfigured the little girl's face. Then she would give a long sigh and say to herself, "It is like a disease. Who can help her? Oh, if our blessed lady could see her only child so disfigured!"

One day Cornelli was astonished to discover that Saturday evening had come again; the last two weeks had gone so fast.

She ran through the garden. Under the plum tree lay the last lovely plums that had ripened into a dark gold. Cornelli picked them up, they were so beautiful to look at, but this year she had found no pleasure in them. She carried the fruit with her and laid it on Martha's table as she entered the cottage.

"Oh, what lovely yellow plums! They must surely taste like pure honey!" exclaimed Dino. "They are from the tree in your garden, aren't they? When the sun shone on it this morning, the fruit glittered on the branches like red-gold. Just like a Christmas tree."

"Yes, they are from that tree. Would you like to eat them?" asked Cornelli

"OH, WHAT LOVELY PLUMS! THEY MUST SURELY TASTE LIKE HONEY!" EXCLAIMED DINO.

CORNELLI, HER CHILDHOOD

"Gladly, but you must have some too," said Dino.

"No, I won't," answered Cornelli. "But you taste them. If you do not care for them, let them be or the birds can have them."

"Oh, there is nothing so sweet and nourishing as these golden plums," declared Dino, eating one after another.

"What a pity I did not know you were so fond of them! You might have told me!" Cornelli said. "Now there are no more left on the tree— these are the last, and they had fallen on the grass. But the pears will soon ripen. They are good, too, even better than the plums. I'll bring you some every day."

"Oh, it would be fine to have a feast of pears every day," said Dino, looking admiringly at the last reddish plum before its destruction. "But that is easy for you to say, Cornelli. You stay right here under the lovely pear tree but I have to journey off in order to sit inside a schoolhouse and bemoan all this freedom that I leave behind."

"You are not going away?" said Cornelli in dismay, for it had never entered her mind that their companionship could have an end.

"Yes, indeed, though I would like to stay here a long time with good Martha. I know of no one so kind except my mother. She takes great care of me."

"Well, everything is over for me when you are gone," said Cornelli in a tone as though Dino were her enemy, and her eyes glistened like glowing coals under the dark hair. She turned away from him as if she would say, "I don't want to hear another word!" but Dino understood her anger.

"No, Cornelli," said he soothingly, "just turn it around, for the very opposite is going to happen. Everything is not over—it has only just started. I have arranged with Martha to come again next summer, and every year after that, until you and I are old and grayheaded."

But Cornelli could not see ahead; the immediate future blinded her. "But it is such a frightfully long time until another summer that you will forget all about me a hundred times over by then!" Cornelli blurted out as though in argument with her companion.

"Oh, no, I will not!" declared Dino calmly. "Not a single time, much less a hundred! I'll prove it to you, Cornelli. Now let us be merry together in the four days that still remain. Each year I will return, and the little kid will grow big enough for us to take a drive together. I'll be coachman and you the lady in the carriage. That will be grand!"

But Cornelli could not be truly merry, for she always saw before her the moment when Dino would say good-bye and her good times would end.

The parting moment came quickly enough, and farewell was taken in Martha's cottage. Cornelli arrived early in the morning, and as Dino drove off, she laid her head on her arms upon the table and wept pitifully, while the saddened Martha sat near her crying quietly.

That evening after dinner was over and Cornelli stood up to leave the room, Miss Dorner said, "You have not spoken a single word all day. You are getting worse instead of better! Must your father find you worse than when he left?"

"Good-night," said Cornelli chokingly, and left the room without looking up.

"There is absolutely nothing to be done with her! You see for yourself, Betty, though you have insisted that little by little there would be a change for the better," said Miss Dorner as

Cornelli closed the door. "Have we, with all our trouble, accomplished nothing? Will she ever make her father happy? Instead of brightening his lonely life, she will bring him trouble and vexation. Did you ever see such obstinacy as the child exhibits?"

"No, I never did," replied Betty. "It seems every word of correction brings exactly the opposite of what we desire. Every time we tell her how hideous she looks she goes to further extremes with her hair. I should like to know how we can break her obstinate will,—whether severity would do it, or whether she needs the companionship of other children who would cure her by ridicule."

"I shall do and say nothing more," concluded Miss Dorner. "My cousin himself shall decide what is to be done with his daughter. But I am sure of one thing: whatever is done, she will never bring happiness to her father."

CHAPTER VII

A FRESH SORROW

AUTUMN came and all the trees in Mr. Hellmut's garden bore heavy burdens of rich-colored fruit. Bright red apples and golden pears showed among the green of the leaves, and dark blue plums, sweet as honey, lay thick under the trees.

Cornelli sat on her bench under the hazelnut tree gazing into space when Matthew came along from the stable. He was wearing his best coat, a sure sign that something special was about to take place.

"Will you come along with me, Cornelli?" he asked, stepping over to where she sat. "I am hitching up the horses for your father comes at eleven o'clock and I am driving down to the lake to meet him. Come along! The bays will be in good trim as they have had a long rest. Do come; it will be fun for you."

Cornelli shook her head.

"No?" said Matthew, plainly disappointed. "Now I thought surely you would be glad to ride out this pleasant morning behind the prancing horses to meet your father. Shall I get some of those pears for you? No again?" Matthew shook his head and went his way. "If our master only had half a dozen boys and as many girls, how lovely it would be on this estate! Then those pears would not be hanging sad and forsaken on the trees," he murmured. "To think of finding no pleasure in driving with two such horses!"

When the time for lessons came, Mr. Mallinger found that all his patience was needed to bear Cornelli's utter indifference. When the two-hour period ended and the carriage bringing her father drew up in front of the house, Mr. Mallinger was astonished that she did not jump up joyfully and run to meet him, but only glanced timidly through the window without even rising.

Cornelli heard her father enter the house and the exclamations of pleasure with which he was greeted by the ladies. She brushed off a tear and went into the room her father had just entered.

"How are you, my child? Here you come at last!" the father exclaimed joyfully, then changing his tone, he continued, "But what a sight, Cornelli!"

She had given him her hand in silence, as she gazed shyly down.

"Whatever is the matter with you?" her father asked. "How queer you look! I would scarcely know you. Push your gypsy hair off your forehead. Aren't you happy at seeing me? Why do you look away? Here I have been looking forward for months to returning home to my daughter who, I thought, would have gained much during my absence. Is this the way I am to find you, Cornelli?" and Mr. Hellmut gazed in sorrowful disappointment at the daughter who evaded his eyes and spoke not a word, but whose face, half hidden by her locks, was so clouded that a rainstorm surely threatened.

"We will discuss it all later, Frederick," said Miss Dorner. "Let us celebrate your homecoming with merriment and put aside sad and troublesome thoughts," and she led her cousin to the table which was spread with all the good things Esther knew her master liked best. But the thoughts of the father were far too troubled for a feast to banish them, and Mr. Hellmut barely touched the delicacies that were served. Ever and again he gazed on his child, who sat before him with bowed head, only now and then casting a timid look toward him. The meal passed with but little gayety, for it was evident Mr. Hellmut forced himself to utter the few words he spoke, and that his mind was filled with disturbing thoughts, and he left the table as soon as he could do so with propriety. ..

"He is going across to the works," said Miss Dorner to her friend, the only one left at the table, for Cornelli forsook the room immediately after her father. "He has had a keen disappointment, and must give vent to his emotion. Seeing the workmen yonder will free him from some of his depression. He will hear much news, and I hope it will be good—of much work and profitable business. It is hard for him to lead a life of such ceaseless activity all for the sake of *such* a child!"

Mr. Hellmut returned hurriedly after a short time, and did not look as though his inspection of the works had calmed him much. Seating himself at the table where the ladies were partaking of coffee, he said, "They have spoiled much for me over there, but I can make the best of that, even though some rather heavy losses do follow. The thing I cannot stand, however, is the change in my child. She makes a horrid appearance, and seems to have grown stupid. She did not show the slightest pleasure at my return, has not spoken a word since I came, has hardly looked at me, and sits there as though she found existence a real misfortune. It is unbearable! What has happened to the child?" and he began to pace the floor in his excitement.

"As far as the child is concerned, nothing has happened. At least we know of nothing, do we, Betty?" said Miss Dorner. "We have both tried to teach her good manners, first of all for your sake, and then because we found she lacked them altogether. But I must be frank, Frederick, even though it gives me pain. Your daughter is so obstinate that absolutely nothing can be done with her. The more we combat it and try to have her form correct habits, the worse everything goes, and the more she persists in her obstinacy. What have we not said about the way she disfigures her face with her hair! All for nothing! The more I said, the more she pulled her hair into her eyes. At last I gave it up, for I saw that only physical punishment could help, and I wished to leave that to you."

Mr. Hellmut paced restlessly up and down the room, and then finally paused to say, "Surely it is possible to control a child of ten years! Is chastising the only way to train a youngster? Can you give me no advice? What is going to happen to the child? A woman surely must know how to rear a child. Something must be done, and at once. I am to blame, for I have neglected her and left her too long in the wrong hands. What would my Cornelia say if she could see her child?" and he threw himself into a chair and hid his face in his hands.

"Calm yourself, Frederick; you are not to blame. Dispositions are dispositions," said Miss Dorner soothingly. "My friend and I have an idea that it might do her good to send her to a boarding-school in the city, where there are a large number of children and young girls. Children help one another more than they know when they live in close contact."

"Do you think that might be good for Cornelli?" the father asked. "The child is not accustomed to the polishing process through ridicule."

"Then for that reason it would make that much more impression," asserted his cousin. "Believe me, this seems to be the only way of breaking the child's obstinacy, if there is a way. If such a school does not conquer her will, nothing in the world can, you may be sure of that, Frederick."

"She is very young to be sent away from home and out among strangers," said the father with feeling. "Yet you may be right, and it seems it must be done, for the child certainly will not grow better here. Have you any suggestions where to send her?"

Miss Dorner said she knew of such a school and offered to take the necessary steps to enter Cornelli for him as soon as she went home. In vain she hoped her cousin's mood would change and that he would become the happy companion of former days. True, he took pains to be an entertaining host to his guests as they sat at the table, but his eyes would roam to the little girl who sat silently at her place. His face would darken with trouble, and one could see what an effort it was for him to take part in the conversation.

At last Miss Dorner decided she had endured

enough of her cousin's trying preoccupation; she would make another attempt to shake him into a little consciousness, so on the third day after his return she said, "It seems as though you are so engrossed, Frederick, that you are forgetful of your duties as host. We are thinking of returning to the city, and perhaps this is in accord with your desire."

"I can easily understand your decision," answered Mr. Hellmut, "for you are right; I *am* as unamiable a host as can be found. But you must comprehend how the change in my child has banished all thought of pleasure, and I can only give attention to one thing—how to help her. I trust that you both will visit my house some other time, when it is more jovial here. You have only to give your order whenever you desire the carriage."

Miss Dorner had not expected this reply and she said angrily, "Really, Frederick, you are going too far! How can any man push aside all else and allow his mind to be so upset on account of such a child?"

"You forget she is my child, and the child of my Cornelia," replied Mr. Hellmut. "We will not discuss it any more, for we would not understand one another and I am far too grateful to you for your good wishes to have any anger creep in at our parting."

Two days later the carriage stood at the door for the ladies and also Miss Mina. She had so ingratiated herself with them both that at her request they had consented to take her to the city with them. She did not wish to live among country people any longer, and one of the ladies was to take her as chambermaid though which of the two was not yet decided. Esther was enraged that Mina should leave such a good home without real reason for, having managed this household since its establishment, she felt the honor of the house was her own. Now, at her master's invitation she stood behind him as he bid farewell to those in the carriage.

Miss Mina gazed out the other side where Cornelli stood. "Won't you give me your hand for the last time? No? That is not very friendly of you," she said in a low tone to the child.

Then Esther spoke up. "Miss Mina," she called out as loudly as she could, "be so kind as to tell the ladies on the journey who it was that stood on the sofa and left the dusty footmarks! It was not children's shoes."

Mina flushed purple-red, and Miss Dorner looked at her in astonishment. She expected a forcible reply, but when none came, she said, "Forward, Matthew!" rather excitedly, for she did not wish any explanation of that incident.

Mr. Hellmut returned to the foundry as the carriage rolled away, and now Cornelli seized Esther's broad hand and pressed it between her own and for the first time in a long while a gleam of pleasure flitted over her face. "Oh, I am so glad you said that! I am so glad! You cannot think how happy it makes me!" she exclaimed quite passionately. "If you had not said that, they would always have believed that I had done it, and had lied when I denied it. But how does Mina know who did it?"

"She knows very well, because she did it herself," replied Esther.

"Oh, oh! Did she do it herself—with her own feet?" cried Cornelli. "Then it is a good thing she is gone. We would much rather be alone, just you and I, Esther. Isn't that so?"

"Indeed, yes!" said the latter, much gratified. "Tell your father about it yourself, and say that I am not afraid of double work, but that I shun snakes in the grass."

CORNELLI, HER CHILDHOOD

Cornelli had scarcely spoken to her father since he returned. She was shy with him, for she knew he disapproved her appearance, yet what could she do? It had to be so. If he discovered what was hidden beneath her hair she was sure he would dislike her still more. Now she wanted to carry Esther's message to him but went into his room slowly and fearfully, not as in the old days when she had burst in upon him when she had something to tell. "It will never be that way again," she mused and the thought lay so heavily on her heart that she paused a moment. And then her father opened the door in front of which she stood.

"Are you here at last, Cornelli?" he asked gladly. "And do you want to pay me a little visit? We have hardly seen one another yet. Come along in! I was just going to fetch you for I wanted to speak to you."

Cornelli stepped in, but said not a word, and did not even look at her father.

"Come, Cornelli," he said, leading her across the room and seating her beside him. "I have something to tell you that should please you. Since I have been away you have changed so much, and not at all to your advantage, so that something must be done. I am going to send you to the city to a boarding-school. There you will live with lots of other children and young girls. You will learn much from them and make friends among them. Both mentally and physically you will become another person and will return home to give joy to your father. I am not pleased with you now, and do not know what is the matter. But things may improve as you become educated. Next week we will make the journey."

Cornelli turned white with fright. At first no sound came from her; then suddenly she burst into a fit of crying.

"Oh, papa," she sobbed, "let me stay at home! I will do right! I will be good! Oh, don't send me to the city among a lot of children! Oh, I can't! Oh, papa, don't send me away!"

"It is for her sake, for her own good," he repeated to himself with conviction, but even with that to strengthen his decision, Cornelli's grief was too much for him, and he made his escape.

When he returned from the foundry at supper time, Esther met him. "I am so glad you have come, Mr. Hellmut," said she excitedly.

"I wanted the child to come down stairs to taste the plum tart I made, for she is exceedingly fond of it, but she only cried out: 'Leave me here! Leave me here!' Alas, Mr. Hellmut, what would we do if Cornelli should sicken and die?"

"Children do not die of obstinacy, Esther."

He wanted to speak harshly, but did not quite

succeed. He ran upstairs to Cornelli's room and found the little girl kneeling beside her bed, her head pressed deep into the pillows, crying as if her heart were broken.

"Oh, don't take me away, papa! Don't take me away!" she pleaded as he entered.

Seeing how she trembled, he said, "I cannot endure this," and left the house in haste.

Mrs. Martha sat in her peaceful little room busy with her work-basket and as she mended she speculated over how matters would go with Cornelli now she was alone with her father—whether the old times would return, or whether something new would be decided about the child's education. And then the door was opened quickly and Mr. Hellmut stepped in.

"I do not know where to turn, Martha!" he exclaimed in an excited manner. "You must stand by me. You knew my wife; you know our child and love her. Tell me, what is the matter with her? Since when has she displayed this terrible obstinacy, or has she always been that way and only grown more self-willed of late? Have you noticed how obstinacy and hardness of heart have taken possession of her during my absence?"

"Things are not very wrong with Cornelli, Mr. Hellmut. She is not a wicked child, I am certain of that." Then she added hastily, "But will you not have a seat?"

He declined it, and kept on pacing to and fro, declaring he was far too disturbed to sit down.

"Cornelli had to change her mode of life too quickly to be able to adapt herself to it," pursued Martha. "Even an older child would have found it difficult and grown a little shy, and Cornelli is still very young. A little plant cannot stand too much pruning all at once. It must have time, and the more delicate the plant, the greater the care that is needed."

"You are not intimating that I have been unwise these last months?" Mr. Hellmut inquired, standing in the middle of the room. "I must look upon it as a blessing that at last she was brought in contact with ladies of culture and good manners, who could awaken in her all that is beautiful, noble and good. My Cornelia would have aroused in her child all the beautiful traits she possessed. But the child bears no resemblance to her, not even in appearance. She has lost everything that used to remind me of her mother."

CORNELLI, HER CHILDHOOD

"If I may be frank, Mr. Hellmut, I would say just this," remarked Martha in her calm manner. "I have always noticed that a little love goes much farther than ever so many precepts. A little child can suffer because of harsh words more than we grown-ups think. We fail to understand the timid creatures and the results that follow our treatment of them. Cornelli has not lost her mother's eyes, even though we are unable to see them since she hides them under her hair."

"That's just it, Martha—this disfigurement and the obstinacy with which she sticks to it! Her timid, indifferent manner changes her entirely. All this tortures, agonizes me. It paralyzes my pleasure, it kills my courage, and blights my hope for the future. It embitters my whole life." Mr. Hellmut spoke with ever increasing excitement. "Now I will help her in the only way I know of; I will put her in a boarding-school, among other children. I have told her about it and she is in utter despair. I cannot bear to see her grief, and it seems to me my Cornelia could have no rest in Heaven if she could see her child crying and pleading so."

"Mr. Hellmut, if you would only keep the

child at home for a little while, to give her a chance to grow calm again!" suggested Martha in a modest tone. "Cornelli has had so many new experiences recently that it would probably be a good thing to let her rest quietly for a time. Meanwhile you could make her understand about the boarding-school, bit by bit, so she would have no dread of it. I would try to help a little by telling her the many good things about such a school and the nice children that attend."

"That is a happy thought, Martha," said Mr. Hellmut, a little soothed. "You will help me by doing what you can to make the prospect pleasing to the child? You are my only help, Martha; remember that!" and with these words Mr. Hellmut went away.

"Dear, oh dear! That good gentleman!" said Martha, following him with her eyes. "What help has he in old, stupid Martha? However, whatever I can do, I will do with pleasure."

Mr. Hellmut went directly to Cornelli's room. The child was kneeling by her bed, and sobbing.

"Stand up, Cornelli, and stop crying," said he. "I meant it all for your good, but you have misunderstood. You shall stay home for a while and perhaps things will look different to you.

In the morning go to Martha, and pay heed to her words. She is your best friend."

Cornelli could not have heard more consoling words. They reawakened hope after the frightful thoughts about going away, and she arose at once. "May I not go at once?" she asked pleadingly.

"Yes, run along," her father answered, "but you have had nothing to eat."

"That does not matter!" exclaimed Cornelli and was already down the stairs.

At last Cornelli was actually running again. She rushed up the steps and into Martha's room.

"I have to go away, Martha, but not just now. But I have to go away, papa says," the child exclaimed. "Can you not help me? Papa told me to come to you—perhaps because I kept crying and he wanted me to stop. But I cannot stop unless you do something so I need not go. I don't want to live among a lot of strange children—I can't! I certainly could not bear it. Oh, how frightful it would be! *Do* help me!"

The dread in Cornelli's voice and the sight of her face, all swollen with weeping, touched Martha's heart.

CORNELLI, HER CHILDHOOD

"Come, Cornelli, sit down on your little stool like in the old days," she said soothingly. "Then I'll tell you something that will help and console you, just as it has helped me when trouble came, and still does. You see, Cornelli, I too have had to go through great affliction, certainly as great as yours today. I had to give a beloved child back to God. I cried out with the pain like you do, and even louder: 'No, I cannot! No, I cannot!' And the more I resisted, the worse I felt, until I thought I really would despair. Then I cried out in my heart: 'Can no one help me?' And all at once I knew who could. I knelt right down and prayed, 'O God, do help me! Help Thou me, for Thou alone canst help!' "

"If I pray like that, I will not have to go away, Martha, will I? Then, dear Lord, help me at once!" exclaimed Cornelli fervently.

"Yes, He will certainly help you," Martha assured her, "but in a way that He knows is best for you. You see, Cornelli, if it is really good for you to go away, and you pray to the Father in Heaven from the bottom of your heart, He will help you so that you will not find living among strangers as hard as you feared it would be. When you have faith in your heart, you can always call on Him for help, and He always gives you aid in the way that is best for you and does you the most good."

"Did you have to give up your child?" Cornelli wished to know.

"Yes, the dear Lord took it to Himself."

"And you could be happy again, Martha?"

"Yes, yes. The pain was great, but I thought only of my child and how happy it was, and of how much suffering it had escaped. The dear Lord taught me to believe He meant well with both my child and me, and then I was able to be happy again."

"I will go now," said Cornelli, standing up suddenly.

"Yes, go home now. You will remember what I have told you?" asked Martha, accompanying her to the door.

"Indeed I will!" she promised, and went running away, as if there was urgent need for haste.

Cornelli had never prayed so earnestly and heartily as she did that day as she knelt at her bed. She confided to her Father in Heaven all her trouble and begged him to be with her and bring happiness to her once more.

CHAPTER VIII

A MOTHER

EVERY morning when Mr. Hellmut sat down to breakfast he found the letters and newspapers that had come in the morning mail at his place.

"Good gracious!" he exclaimed on the morning following the events in the last chapter. "What correspondence have you in the city, Cornelli? Here is a letter for you."

Cornelli glanced incredulously at the letter.

"It is really yours. It is addressed to Miss Cornelli Hellmut, Illerbach, The Iron Foundry," said her father, reading the address. "There, take it!"

Cornelli opened the envelope eagerly and read:

"Dear Cornelli:

"Just think, I have been sick and have had to lie in bed. The doctor has forbidden me to read and to write, so this must be a very short letter. It is awfully tedious for me, for the other children are away at school all day, and mama always has so much to do. Mux is a most useless little fellow. Could you not pay me a visit? It would please me immensely. You would be able to tell me so much about Illerbach and Mrs. Martha. I love her as much as a grandmother. And you could tell me about your little kid, and Matthew, and about the fine horses and, above all else, about yourself. The days when you came to Mrs. Martha's house when I was there were so merry that I would be happy to have a visit from you. Do come, I beg you, and that soon!

"Your friend,
Dino."

As Cornelli folded the letter her father asked, "May I also read it?" so Cornelli immediately handed it over to him.

"Who is this friend who wants you to visit him so much?" asked the father in astonishment. "I expect you will begin to cry again, for a visit to him will mean that you go to the city."

"Oh, no, papa! I would like to go very much indeed. It is Dino, who was with Martha."

The father put down his spoon and gazed at his daughter in surprise. "How you puzzle me, Cornelli!" said he at last. "Here you are wanting to visit a strange family. You do not know one of them except this boy. Yet you have no scruples about going—no timidity at all."

"Dino knows me. He knows I am coming only to see him, and he will manage it so I do not have to see his mother and his sisters. He knows all about it," was Cornelli's explanation.

"That explains nothing to me," returned the father curtly, picking up his papers.

Shortly afterward he stepped into Martha's house. "Here I am again, Martha! What do you think?" he called out to her. "Here is a letter bringing Cornelli an invitation to visit the boy who stayed with you. What about him? Who are his parents?"

At this question Martha bubbled over with praise of Dino. She had never seen a boy so polite as he, nor one so thoughtful and friendly toward the humblest people. He was exceptionally well trained and had a fine education, yet so simple as to become sincerely attached to aged, humble Martha! She had never read letters so beautiful, so loving, so elevating as those that came from the mother to the son. He always read them aloud to her, and each one had moved her to tears.

"Martha," at last interrupted Mr. Hellmut, "I conclude from what you say that it would be a fortunate thing for my daughter to spend even one day with such a family."

"Oh, sir, it would afford me great pleasure if you would take her there. I could know no greater!" and Martha wiped her eyes.

"You shall have that pleasure, Martha, for we will go tomorrow, and you shall have a report in the evening how matters went," said Mr. Hellmut, and shaking her hand he departed.

As he passed the garden bench where his daughter sat musing, he called out, "Get everything ready, Cornelli, for tomorrow we're off to the city. Esther will wake you early—at six o'clock."

"I'll call her punctually," sounded Esther's voice through one of the open windows, for she was a good housewatch and always seemed to hear everything that went on in the house and garden.

Early the next morning the shiny bays trotted down the valley. They kept a steady pace for four hours, but that was only a pleasure to them.

Cornelli sat in her corner of the carriage lost in thought. She was wondering how she could tell the maid on their arrival that she wished to see only Dino, that she wanted to be taken straight to his room. Then she pondered how she would forbid Dino to call his mother and sisters, for she wanted to see only him. She would have a long visit with Dino and then quietly slip away without anyone noticing her departure. She had many things to tell Dino, but first of all he must hear that at last it was known who had stood on the sofa, for she had confided to him the deep resentment and grief she had borne so long.

So they arrived in the city much sooner than Cornelli had expected, and ere she was aware the carriage drew up in front of the hotel at which her father usually stopped.

"Shall I come back in four hours?" she asked as she jumped down. "I know the way, for Dino has described it to me."

"Wait a moment! That won't do! I am coming with you," said Mr. Hellmut.

That was not at all according to the way Cornelli had planned it, but she could not object.

Dino had given his address in the letter, and as Mr. Hellmut knew his way about the city, they walked quickly down one street and then another until they turned onto a narrow street where stood the house they sought. Together they climbed four flights of stairs, and at last stood before the door.

"If the inhabitants are like their dwelling, we will not spend much time up here," Mr. Hellmut said, looking with misgiving at the awkward entrance.

"Dino is not like this," answered Cornelli quickly, for although she did not quite understand what her father meant, she felt his words were an attack on her friend.

"Climb up, Cornelli, and pull the bell-cord hanging there," ordered her father.

Cornelli obeyed and a slender young girl, a little taller than Cornelli, opened the door. She looked out of a pair of dark, earnest eyes in surprise at the new arrivals. Cornelli drew back, but her father stepped forward saying, "What we see is not so frightful. How do you do, my child? Is your mother in, and may I speak with her a moment?"

It was Nika who had opened the door and now with the utmost politeness she led the gentleman into the room and said she would fetch her mother immediately.

At Nika's polite invitation Mr. Hellmut seated himself in an armchair and looked around the small but well arranged room which was brightened with many charming paintings.

As Nika went toward the door, Cornelli said to her in a low tone, "I wish to visit Dino."

"Come, I'll show you the way," sounded a little voice from behind the door, for Mux had quickly hidden himself there and had been peeping at the newcomers with inquisitive eyes. Now he came forward and, taking Cornelli's hand, drew her along with him. The mother had heard the strange voices, and now entered from another room.

"She's not like her surroundings either," thought Mr. Hellmut as he rose to introduce himself. "Following your son's invitation, I have brought my daughter, Mrs. Halm," said he. "With your permission she can stay with her sick friend a few hours, and then she will return to me at my hotel."

"I am very grateful to you for your kindness," replied the lady. "My son has looked forward to her visit with great pleasure. Cornelli showed him so many kindnesses while he was alone at Illerbach that we feel we know her and love her already. He is very grateful, and so am I. Might I not beg that she be allowed to stay for a few days, or at least the entire day?"

"You are most kind, Mrs. Halm," answered Mr. Hellmut, rather astonished that his shy child had given the boy so much pleasure. "It is just out of politeness," said he to himself, and aloud, "That cannot be, for my daughter would not stay. She is very shy, and has all sorts of peculiar ways, as you must have noticed."

"I certainly would not keep Cornelli against her wish, but if the child's wishes coincide with ours, may I have your permission?"

Mrs. Halm had such a persuasive way that Mr. Hellmut would have granted anything she asked, and this request was really pleasing to him, so he said, "Certainly, Mrs. Halm, for it would be a great pleasure to me. What better thing could I wish for my child than for her to know you and your daughters? But I am convinced she will want to return with me. Please accept my heartiest thanks for your friendliness, for to spend even a day in your house will do the child good."

Mr. Hellmut said farewell and departed. As he stepped out of the house into the street a girl carrying school-books and bag collided with him with such violence that he opened his arms and caught her in them. It was Agnes's way to plunge ahead, and now both of them burst out into hearty laughter.

"You also belong to Mrs. Halm?" he asked, looking down approvingly into the fresh face

and wide open eyes so full of life. How neat, how refined the child was!

"Yes, of course!" was the quick answer as Agnes ran on her way.

"Oh, happy mother! What a fortunate woman!" said Mr. Hellmut to himself. "Oh, the difference between my Cornelli and these girls!" and he hastened his steps as though he would run away from thoughts which caused him such anguish.

Dino always confided everything to his mother, and had therefore described his sojourn at Illerbach in detail and had told about his companionship with Cornelli. He did not omit telling about the little girl's strange affliction, but he had his mother's promise to keep this secret to herself. It did not seem wrong to Dino that his mother should know about it—she knew everything he did. Therefore when the invitation had been sent to Cornelli, Mrs. Halm had given strict orders that if she came no remarks were to be made about the way she wore her hair; they were to show no surprise whatever, to take no notice of it.

Little Mux was much elated to have a new companion. He looked upon Cornelli as an old acquaintance, Dino had talked about her so much. Now he led her to the kitchen.

"Surely Dino is not in bed out here," said Cornelli in surprise.

"No, this is the kitchen; there are no beds here," said Mux, "but I want to show you first of all why Agnes cried today for a whole hour, perhaps two," and he led his new companion to a large pile of apple parings that lay in the garbage bucket. "And now you see how silly Agnes is to cry so when apple pie comes afterward."

"But why did she cry?" asked Cornelli in quick sympathy.

"We don't know," replied Mux.

"Why didn't the housemaid pare the apples?"

"There is no maid, only stupid Trine," Mux informed her.

"Who is stupid Trine?"

"She has to help; she is small and fat," Mux said, describing her. "Mama has to show her how to cook, and she has to fetch what we need, only she always brings the wrong thing. Then Dino says: 'That is stupid Trine, we must send her away.' And mama says: 'Trine has to live, too.' And they do not send her away."

Cornelli felt great sympathy for Agnes. She thought that she also probably had a great sorrow; she would not be afraid of her, as she was of the proud sister who had opened the door.

"I am sure your other sister never cries, does she, Mux? Are you not afraid of her?"

"No, not a little bit, not even the tiniest little bit," Mux assured her. "She makes a face as if she would like to cry, and a thousand times she begins to cry, nobody knows why."

Instantly Cornelli's fear of Nika changed to sympathy. If she cried and never told why, perhaps her sorrow was the greatest of all.

"Now let us go to Dino," said she, hurrying to the door that the little fellow had pointed out.

"Oh, wait, for first I want to show you the big picture book. You will just love it!" he declared. "And there is something in it that looks just like you—an owl. It has hair over its eyes like you. But you must not speak about it, for mama has forbidden it."

"No, I do not wish to see the book. Take me to Dino," urged Cornelli.

"But you must see it later," asserted Mux. "There are many pretty things in it. You will find you will always want to look at that book again," and he opened a door into Dino's room.

"So you have come at last, Cornelli!" Dino called out as he sat up in his bed, and looked happily toward her.

Cornelli was overjoyed at seeing him once more and seated herself on his bed and quickly

began to tell all about what had happened at
Illerbach since he had left. Dino had so many
questions to ask that neither noticed how the
time flew. Mux soon disappeared, for since he
could not claim the entire attention of his new
friend, he preferred to see what preparations
were afoot for the next meal.

Now Mrs. Halm stepped into her son's room,
and taking Cornelli's hand she said, "My dear
child, I have hardly had a look at you yet, but I
thought you and Dino would like to be undisturbed for awhile, so you could talk about your
friends and your experiences at Illerbach. I am
sure Dino has thoroughly enjoyed your visit.
Now come with me to dinner. Then Dino will
have to sleep a little while, after which he surely
will want you to come back to him again."

That was a difficult moment for Cornelli. She
had hoped to spend the whole day alone with
Dino. Now she had to sit at table with his
mother and two sisters. But Mux was her consolation; he was so cunning. She was aware she
was different from these children and far less
attractive than the dainty Nika. Even though
this pretty girl did not show it, Cornelli was
sure she must be filled with disgust, for even

little Mux had seen her peculiarity at once and in his outspoken way had remarked about it. And now Agnes would be there too. Both of them had a sorrow which made Cornelli feel there was a bond between them, and it gave her the needed courage to follow Mrs. Halm who stood waiting at the door. Agnes stood expectantly in the middle of the room as Cornelli entered, and immediately came toward the guest and shook her hand.

"I am so glad you came, Cornelli," she said gaily. "Dino has spoken about you so much that we all wanted to know you."

"I'll sit next to you," said Mux, and dragged his chair alongside of Cornelli's.

"You stick to your own post; this is my place," declared Agnes, and to make her meaning clear pushed back both chair and boy.

Mrs. Halm had gone into the kitchen, so he could not call on her for help, and this increased his anger.

"Yes, yes, you always want to order everyone around!" he cried savagely. "And once you broke a person on the wheel."

Just then the mother stepped into the room, and Agnes exclaimed, "Oh, mama, Mux is saying terrible things! Ought he not to be in bed?"

Mux was gathering all his forces to protest against this suggested punishment, but Mrs. Halm quelled the little tempest with the words, "No, no. Today Cornelli is among us for the first time, and it is a holiday. So Mux shall not be sent to bed, but he must sit quietly in his chair and say grace for us; then everything will be all right."

Immediately the meal was over, Nika and Agnes had to hurry back to school, and Mrs. Halm had to oversee Trine's work, so she suggested that Mux entertain Cornelli a while. That was just what he wanted, and he said triumphantly, "Now I will show you that Agnes really broke someone on the wheel."

"Oh, Mux, I do not believe that!"

"You can read all about it. See, it says so there, don't you see?" and Mux placed his big picture book on Cornelli's lap and pointed to a beautiful picture on the page where he had opened it. "Now read; there it is. Dino once read it aloud and so I know it."

Cornelli read aloud: "Agnes had Rudolf von Warth broken on the wheel."

"Now you see it yourself!" repeated Mux.

Cornelli did not know just what the picture meant, so she started to read the story that explained it. She read on and on, more eager each moment. It was all so vividly described that she devoured page after page.

"Now you know," said Mux a little impatiently. "Do look at the little goat-cart."

"But I would like to finish reading the story, and I would like to know how it all came—" But Mux had turned the page.

"But, Mux," continued Cornelli, "this is quite another Agnes, a queen. You must no longer believe it was your sister Agnes who committed such a frightful deed."

"Well, look at the goat-cart!" demanded Mux impatiently.

"Why is the child weeping so by the roadside? See how he presses his hands into his eyes! Oh, he is in such misery! Do you know why?"

Mux shook his head.

"Then I must read about it quickly," she declared, and was soon so deep in the story that she did not notice how Mux tugged at her, pressed against her and finally shook the book in his effort to stop her reading.

His mother came into the room, saying, "Dino

has shortened his nap a little, and is asking for you, Cornelli. Will you come?"

Instantly Cornelli closed the book for she was anxious to return to Dino. She glanced regretfully at the book, for she would have liked to know the outcome of the story.

"So the book pleases you?" said Mrs. Halm noticing Cornelli's longing glance. "It has been the joy of all my children from the oldest to the youngest. You can look at it again."

But Dino had so many things to talk over with Cornelli that the time passed away much more quickly than expected, and the first thing they knew, Mux came running with the news that Cornelli should come to supper; they were serving it early because she had to leave immediately afterward.

"Mux, bring mother here," said Dino, and the youngster ran off on the errand. "Would you not like to stay with us, Cornelli?" continued Dino. "At least a few days? It would be so jolly! You will, will you not?" he urged.

Cornelli experienced a strange emotion. She was afraid to say yes; she simply could not believe that everybody in this house was ready to be her friend—that they wanted to keep her there. They would not continue to want her if she stayed and they came to know her. Mrs. Halm came in with Mux, who had already informed her that Cornelli was going to stay, that Dino would not let her go.

"Then you will stay with us, Cornelli? I hear you have said yes," said Mrs. Halm, highly pleased. "I was going to propose it, but now that Dino has already arranged it with you, it is just as well. You know your father gave permission for you to stay and all I have to do is to send him word. Now there is no hurry about supper."

Mrs. Halm went off to write a note to Mr. Hellmut which the little fat Trine set off to carry to the hotel.

Cornelli seated herself again beside Dino with a feeling half of pleasure, half of fear. Noticing her pensiveness, Dino asked, "Aren't you glad to stay with us? Oh, if you only knew how glad I am!"

"Why, certainly I am glad to stay with you, Dino," Cornelli assured him, "and also with Mux. Your mother is so good to me too, but I am afraid of your two sisters, they are so different from me. I just have to think all the time how it must be for stupid Trine when she does everything wrong and does not know how to do otherwise. I know only too well how it is when one is stupid."

Dino gave a little laugh as he asked, "How did Trine get into your mind? Don't you worry about her; mama takes good care of her."

Cornelli said no more, but Dino knew that she was still pondering the matter.

After a short while Mrs. Halm informed them it was time for Dino to rest again; that the morrow would bring more happy companionship.

Cornelli followed Mrs. Halm back to the room where the two sisters sat at their work and Mux was bending over his book. Behind them came the half-grown Trine with a basket on her arm. As she passed Nika's chair the basket caught on it and Trine gave such a sharp tug at it that Nika received quite a jolt.

"You are getting more clumsy all the time," exclaimed Nika crossly.

Cornelli flushed as though the rebuke was intended for her, for she thought Nika deemed her as clumsy as Trine. The servant-girl offered no excuse, but in her embarrassment was more awkward than ever. Cornelli understood her perfectly for that was the way she herself acted, she knew.

"Now let us sit down to supper," said the mother, "and when the children have finished their work afterward, we will sing a little. You sing too, Cornelli, do you not?"

"I am sure I do not know the songs, so I will not be able to," she answered timidly.

When the supper was ended Mux made a dash for his book and carried it to Cornelli, for he wanted to continue the conversation they had begun over its pages, but his mother had other intentions.

"No," she said; "give your book to Cornelli, for it is time for you to go to bed. You can join us tomorrow."

Mux went with reluctance, and as his mother led him away he said to Cornelli, "Don't you go away until I come back!"

Cornelli felt embarrassed the moment confiding little Mux disappeared, for she was left alone with the two sisters for the first time. What would happen? But the two girls were so buried in their work that neither of them raised a head, and Cornelli picked up the book. There were lovely stories in it, and she was eager to learn how the one she had begun ended. She read more and more. As soon as she finished one, a new picture would lure her on to another.

Suddenly Cornelli was startled by the sound of sweet music close beside her. Agnes was at the piano. Cornelli could read no more, for Agnes played one lovely tune after another with such ease that it seemed a pure joy. Yet she was only a year older than Cornelli, for Dino had told her. She sat listening to the wonderful melodies with the greatest rapture, and Mrs. Halm found her so when she returned to the room after she had made her usual bedtime visit to Dino.

"Mama," called out Agnes to her gayly, "I am happy to play all the joyful music I know because I have finished my great composition."

"That's good, Agnes. And how is the painting coming along, Nika?" asked Mrs. Halm.

Nika replied complainingly that she had been unable to do as much as she wished, the days were always too short, and she could do nothing by lamplight; but her mother ought to see how very little remained to be done on the picture. "Just another hour of daylight and it would have been finished," she said as she placed a large picture under the light of the lamp.   It was a large painting, much like those which hung on the walls of the room.   Cornelli had never seen such wonderful colors as the artist had spread on this canvas.   Red roses were hanging over an ancient wall and over the high ruins dense ivy crept, with its glossy green shoots.   An old oak tree stretched its great branches over the ruined wall, and a clear stream flowed peacefully toward a meadow where red and blue flowers nodded as though greeting it.

Cornelli gazed on the beautiful picture; she had never seen such work, and she imagined she could hear the stream as it rippled on its way through the meadow, it was so lifelike.   And Nika had painted it!   It seemed to Cornelli that there was a great, deep gulf between her and the two sisters, dividing them forever and ever.

Cornelli remained silent, even though Mrs. Halm urged her to join in the singing as much as she was able, and she could have done so because the evening hymn they sang had been taught her by Martha.   The day had brought her so many new, so many deep impressions that she felt she could utter no note, and the timid little girl withdrew from all participation in the family activity. When the hymn was ended, Agnes jumped up suddenly, exclaiming, "Oh, mother, it's no use! When you are hoarse and Dino is in bed, our singing is frightful. Nika chirps like a hen with its throat cut."

"Then we must stop singing," said Nika, shrugging her shoulders like an aristocrat.

"No, the singing must be done by the entire household, otherwise it has no value," declared Agnes. "To think that the most beautiful custom is so little followed!"

Mrs. Halm went over to Cornelli, and taking her by the hand in her kindly way, she said, "You are tired, dear child; I can see that. I will take you to your tiny bedroom. A door opens into the room where Nika and Agnes sleep," she continued, as she stood in the little room with Cornelli. "You may leave it open if you like, and all three of you will be practically in one room." Then bidding Cornelli a hearty good-night, she wished her sound sleep the first night under her roof.

Nika and Agnes gave her a short: "Good-night," and then Cornelli was alone in her room. She had no desire to open the door, for her awe of the sisters was now greater than when she first arrived. How high above her they stood!

What had Agnes meant by the most beautiful thing in the world? Perhaps singing; but that was by no means the most beautiful. Surely the loveliest thing was a painting like Nika's, with such roses and trees, such a meadow with limpid waters. At last Cornelli's eyes closed, though she still saw the roses, and thought they looked up at Nika in adoration as she stood beside her so tall and beautiful, quite like a queen, and Cornelli thought: "Oh, if she would say just a single kind word to me!" Then Nika did turn toward her and say: "You are a clumsy, stupid Cornelli!" But Cornelli saw all this in a dream.

In the next room Agnes was saying to her sister: "If only Cornelli would say something! One can never tell what is in her mind. How could Dino find her amusing and make such a close friend of her? She just sits there and never says a word."

"That is not the least of it," replied Nika. "It is really horrid of her that she should make herself look like a savage islander. I don't understand why mama doesn't push that long hair back off her face."

CHAPTER IX

A GREAT CHANGE

NEXT morning Mux had scarcely opened his eyes before he asked if he might carry his book to Cornelli, for that had been the agreement the night before. However, he had first to submit to his usual morning fate, but at last ran off, his hair smoothly combed and his cheeks glowing like red apples. Sure enough, there sat Cornelli in a corner of the living-room listening intently while Agnes practiced her music lesson. He rushed up to her, and found the book already in her lap.

"Oh, now we'll have a whole day of reading and storytelling!" he exulted gleefully. "The others will soon have to go to school."

But Mux had forgotten for the very first time that breakfast came first. The two girls left immediately after, and Dino gave a signal by knocking on his wall that he wished Cornelli to come to him. Mux made a great fuss about it, and would not cease until Cornelli had promised to spend all the hours when Dino had to sleep

191

with him. He was still grumbling as she left the room, and she was both thrilled and astonished at the thought that anyone liked her so much. On entering Dino's room he asked if she would not read aloud to him, since she was so happy to read to Mux out of his picture book.

"Have you such interesting stories too?" asked Cornelli, hesitating as she called to memory her own lovely books in which there had been so many unintelligible things that she preferred to leave them alone.

"Yes indeed, I think so. Just see for yourself," said Dino. "Take down that book called 'Merry Trips.' There are pictures in it too, though not so large as in Mux's book and these are not colored, but they are so comical that they keep you laughing."

Cornelli took down the book and soon afterwards one peal of laughter and another filled the room, so that Mrs. Halm said to herself with a smile of satisfaction, "No, no, everything is not lost yet!"

And thus the week passed: Cornelli spent most of the time reading aloud, first with Dino, then with Mux, and hour by hour she herself grew more eager about it, so that when Mux

CORNELLI, HER CHILDHOOD

MRS. HALM STEPPED INTO DINO'S ROOM JUST AS CORNELLI
FINISHED READING A STORY WHICH HAD SET BOTH
OF THEM LAUGHING.

wished to play soldiers, she would say, "You can do that alone. Let me read and then I will tell you all about it afterward," and so the thick book was soon read through. She did not become much better acquainted with the girls; indeed, Nika had scarcely spoken to her.

On Saturday evening Mrs. Halm stepped into Dino's room just as Cornelli finished reading a story which had set both of them laughing aloud.

"How are you getting along, children?" she asked. "Cornelli's father expects to hear from me tomorrow morning, saying whether he is to take her home or leave her with us another week. It is for Cornelli herself to decide, for of course all of us wish to keep her."

"Don't go! Don't go! Tell him he must not come for a long while," urged Mux, who had slipped into the room behind his mother and now held on to Cornelli as though her father were trying to drag her away.

"No, no, Cornelli, you won't leave us yet," chimed in Dino. "Tomorrow I am to get up for the first time, and you must be here to see if I can walk. Afterward you must stay with us until I can go to school again, isn't that so, Cornelli?"

"You must not press Cornelli too much," said his mother. "Perhaps she wishes to go home, and your pleading keeps her from saying so."

But all this urging by both the boys gave Cornelli such joy that there was no doubt in her mind what she wished to do, and she said, "I would be very glad to remain."

"Oh, how fine!" exclaimed Dino. "And, mama, do beg for another two or even three weeks. It is so good to have Cornelli here."

"I shall ask Mr. Hellmut to allow her to remain with us longer," returned Mrs. Halm, "but I must not determine the time: her father will do that."

"Yes, 'longer' is just the word to use, for then one can always beg for more time, and say that is what we meant by 'longer'," said Dino.

That day when Dino's time for sleep arrived and Cornelli was sitting with Mux, the two were so happy over the prospect of being together for a while longer that Mux opened the piano and asked Cornelli to play, saying they would sing together. Cornelli explained she could not play but she would sing if he would suggest a song.

"You sing one, and then perhaps I can," he proposed.

CORNELLI, HER CHILDHOOD

Cornelli was in just the humor to sing once again, and she began in her full, clear voice while he listened in rapt admiration:

"Snow on the meadow,
Snow on the tiles,
Snow all around us,
Life is all smiles.
Hurrah! Hurrah!
Life is all smiles.

"The sun's in the heavens;
O birds, start your song;
Flowers by the brookside,
Let's hurry along.
Hurrah! Hurrah!
Let's hurry along.

"The swallows' returning,
The birds singing gay,
Proclaim that the springtime
Is now on the way.
Hurrah! Hurrah!
Is now on the way."

Suddenly the door flew open and Agnes rushed in.

"But why do you never speak a word?" she cried out as she entered. "Just to think of it! Why do you never say anything, Cornelli?"

"What should I have said?" asked Cornelli, greatly shocked.

"Don't be frightened," said Mux to calm her. "I'll help you if she tries to hurt you!"

"Don't be so absurdly stupid, Mux!" exclaimed his sister as she went on toward the kitchen and met her mother who stood in the doorway. "Did you hear it, mother? Come along and get Cornelli to sing that song over again."

"Well did I hear it and with both joy and wonder," said Mrs. Halm, stepping over to Cornelli. "You have a voice, dear child, that we would like to hear again. You will sing with us this evening, Cornelli? Now we know how your voice sounds, you should not hesitate."

"When I am nervous I cannot sing correctly, and it certainly does not sound well," replied Cornelli.

"But why should you be nervous?" asked the mother. "You know us all quite well now."

"Because I am not like Agnes and Nika and cannot do the things they do," explained Cornelli, as she drew her forehead into a frown in the old manner.

"You just stay with me, then you will never be nervous," said Mux protectingly. "I am afraid of no one in the whole world—only of the dark," he added, as he saw Cornelli's eyes searching him and he felt she could see through him. "No, not even of the dark if you are with me," he declared victoriously.

Agnes returned from her school work earlier than usual that afternoon, and she dashed to the piano immediately she was in the room, calling, "Come along, Cornelli! Now comes our singing. Mux must entertain himself for awhile. Now I will sing the first stanza of this song alone, and then you will do it with me," Agnes said, and began *"The Moon Has Risen."*

"Oh, I learned that song long ago! Shall I sing second voice at once?" asked Cornelli.

"What! Can you sing second voice? Can you really? That would be fine! Just sing away!"

So the pair sang on together, for Nika had not finished her work, and the time for the evening song when the mother always joined them had not yet arrived. Now and then Mrs. Halm came into the room, but Nika was so deeply absorbed in her task that the music did not disturb her, though Agnes was putting the new voice through many a test. Cornelli lost all self-consciousness and sang with the full vigor of her clear, strong voice. Agnes grew more and more zealous, and it really did sound as if a full choir were in the room. At last Mrs. Halm entered the room again and Nika stopped her work, looked up in astonishment and listened. When the song was ended, Agnes clapped her hands for joy.

"Your voice is clear as a bell, Cornelli!" she exclaimed. "Oh, if I only had such a voice! What would I not sing! Do you know many songs? Just name all you know."

Cornelli turned the pages of the song book and found she knew quite a number.

Agnes was enraptured. "Now our evening singing will not be a chirping any more. Now we will have something different—quite different!" she declared enthusiastically, and rushed to her music rack as she conceived a new idea. She selected some more pieces, all of them for two voices which she had used in taking her music lessons, but never at home, for Nika could not join her.

"Come along, Cornelli, try to sing after me. Then I will sing my own part, and you will sing yours. See, there are the notes for your part," Agnes explained, and thereupon began to sing.

Cornelli did not read music easily, for Mr. Mallinger had never given her much instruction along that line. But she had an ear for music and could immediately repeat an air she had once heard. First they started with the easiest song and Cornelli grasped the melody immediately. She quickly noted where to pause and where to join in again. They passed on to a second song and then to a third.

"Once again! Just once more!" urged Agnes over and over, for each time proved better than the last. Finally the songs went so well that Agnes jumped up from her stool in ecstasy. "You are a wonderful Cornelli!" she declared. "Who would have thought it? Don't go back home yet! Stay with us awhile longer and we will sing every day. Did you hear us, mama?"

The mother said she had and that Dino had asked to have his door left open.

"What do you say to our studying a duet together early tomorrow morning, and greeting Dino with it when he comes back to this room?"

Cornelli was quite willing.

Then Mrs. Halm requested them to sing an evening hymn as usual at the close of the day; she had postponed this hour far beyond the ordinary time on account of the girls' happy occupation. Agnes asserted they ought not to choose a mild hymn—they must sing a mighty song of praise and thanksgiving, and her suggestion brought the assent of the others.

Cornelli was so overwhelmed with the unexpected joy of Agnes's friendship that she had to sit on her bed musing a long time. She wondered why she could not be really happy when everybody in the house was so good to her. At last she decided it was because of the old fear that still possessed her that she looked different from everybody else, and that her horns would continue to grow until she could conceal them no longer. Then everyone would think as Mux had, even though they did not say it.

The next morning when Cornelli had just gotten out of bed, Mrs. Halm stepped into her room and taking her by the hand said kindly, "Cornelli, you give us all so much pleasure! You have afforded my sick Dino many happy hours and you have entertained little restless Mux so well that now he could scarcely live without you. I want to do something for you. I should like to make you look lovely and to do away with what disfigures you," and she started to arrange the child's hair.

"Oh, no, no!" Cornelli protested. "Then it

is all over! I must go home—I want to go home!
They will all laugh at me, and won't be able to
endure me! Oh, you don't know what is the
matter!"

"I know everything, my dear child," said the
mother calmly. "Dino has told me. You know
that I love you, Cornelli; do you not? and you
know I would not cause you pain, or do anything
that was not for your good. You are suffering
from a deception that I would cure."

"No, no, it is no deception; certainly it is not!"
exclaimed Cornelli, thoroughly alarmed. "Miss
Dorner told me of it, and so did Miss Grideelen.
They saw it, and I know it. Oh, don't push my
hair aside!"

"Cornelli," continued Mrs. Halm quietly, "the
ladies told you they saw little horns on your
forehead that will keep getting larger if you per-
sist in wrinkling your brows into a heavy frown.
That is the way you understood it, but not the
way they meant it. They wanted to say that
when you wrinkle up your forehead so, you
look as though you had little horns, and they said
it to stop you from doing that. They meant well
by you; only you have misunderstood them. But
you understand me and know I only seek your

good. Let me do the thing I know will cure you.
Surely you have faith in me?"

Cornelli groaned, but only a little.

With skillful hands the mother had continued
working with the hair and now it was nicely
parted and thick brown waves framed the fore-

head that was snow-white because no ray of sun-shine had touched it all the summer long. She braided it into two thick plaits and twisted them around Cornelli's head so that they made quite a crown, and with a smile she looked down into Cornelli's face, for the change she had wrought filled her mother heart with pleasure.

"Now come with me and we will see if the children notice the change," and she took Cornelli's hand to lead her out.

Cornelli was glad enough to have Mrs. Halm step into the room with her for she would not have dared to go alone, and even now she looked shyly down on the floor as the door opened. Mux had been impatiently waiting for his companion, and ran to meet her. "What have you done, Cornelli?" he asked, suddenly stopping in won-der. "You look quite neat, and so pretty about the forehead, and you have bright eyes like a canary bird. You don't look like an owl any more."

"Why, Cornelli, you are quite transformed!" Agnes exclaimed. "Let me have a look! Stand aside a little, Mux! No, one would never know you! It was a happy thought to do that, for now it's a real joy to look at you."

"Mrs. Halm did it," said Cornelli, quite confused over the compliment.

Nika gazed at Cornelli and said, "You are another girl! How did it come about?"

These words were spoken in such a captivating tone that a deep thrill of satisfaction went through Cornelli. She tried to suppress it, for it did not seem possible that she should be rid of her frightful distress forever.

Now Agnes urged Cornelli to begin practicing their song, so that when Dino arose they could accord him a festive reception. Cornelli quickly agreed and the exercises began and were repeated again and again, for Agnes could never weary of undertaking new duets—pieces she had never been able to try before because of the lack of a second voice.

Dino did not appear until dinner, and though he was still pale he was very lively. "Hurrah, Cornelli!" he exclaimed as he entered the living-room. "Now you look just like you did at Illerbach when you forgot you had to draw your curtain over your forehead. You look even better than then! How good you are to look at, Cornelli! Hurrah again, and joy unequaled!"

But now Dino had a second surprise. Suddenly the festival song was begun and Cornelli's voice rang out so pure and full that Dino nudged Nika and whispered: "Do you hear? Now you see! Now do you admit it?" And one could easily see that heretofore these two had not held the same opinion of Cornelli.

The day was truly a festive one. Cornelli's natural cheerfulness asserted itself and incited all the others to such happiness that the mother herself gazed in joyous astonishment on her two daughters who seldom had shown such unclouded joy. Added to this was her Dino's beaming countenance.

"Wasn't I right?" Dino said to his sisters, after Cornelli had retired and the family was separating for the night, for often since Cornelli had come one or the other had said to him on the quiet, "We cannot conceive what you find attractive or amusing in Cornelli."

Alone in her room, Cornelli felt as though she was in a dream. Whatever had happened to her? Could it actually be true the great affliction which had oppressed her so long and taken all the joy out of her life was gone all at once and forever? Mrs. Halm had declared it was all a mistake and the children had proven it was so.

206

CORNELLI, HER CHILDHOOD

It must be true she was the old Cornelli and could be happy again with no fear lurking in her heart. How filled with joy and gratitude she was!

"Oh, God has been very good to me in every way!" she said in her heart. She remembered how she had prayed to Him when she was grieving because she was to be sent to the city. Now He had let her come to the city, but in such a vastly different way from the one she had so feared. Just by coming her greatest trouble was taken away. Yes, Martha was quite right; she would not forget it; she would never again try to force matters but always beg the dear God to do with her according to His will.

"I have some special news for you, Cornelli," said Mrs. Halm the next day as the family gathered for supper. "As you know, I wrote to your father the other day begging him to allow you to stay with us a little longer. He has replied, and says that he would be glad to have his little daughter stay with us for a whole year and share in all the lessons my daughters take. But you are to write to your father yourself, Cornelli, and tell him just how you feel about this suggestion."

"Oh, you must stay with us, Cornelli! You will remain with us, won't you?" Dino pleaded. "Stay here until summer, and then I will go to Illerbach with you. I am going back to dear Martha; that is all settled."

"I too!" said Mux with determination. "And

you know, Cornelli," he whispered in her ear, "I will stay with you at your house, and Dino can go alone to old Martha."

Agnes was enchanted with the prospect. "Oh, how grand, how grand!" she ejaculated time and again. "Now we will take singing lessons together, learn the same songs and sing them at home. That will be unutterable joy!" And even Nika added: "Do write your father that you want to stay with us, Cornelli. We really have only begun to know you."

Cornelli's eyes sparkled with ever-increasing joy. Everybody desired to keep her—*everybody!* Then another thought occurred to her: When her father had wished to leave her in the city a whole year, it was boarding-school he had had in mind for her. How different everything was from what she had expected and dreaded!

"Oh, I should dearly love to stay, dearly!" she said suddenly in a warm impulse. "May I write to papa at once?"

Two days later when Mr. Hellmut was sitting down to breakfast he opened a bulky letter from the city before he looked at the other correspondence lying at his hand. The envelope contained two letters, and he read first one and then the other in surprise. Mrs. Halm wrote that every member of her family had received his proposal concerning Cornelli with jubilation, for the little girl had won all their hearts, and her departure would make a great gap in her family. Cornelli's letter read as follows:

"Dear Father:

I would so love to stay here. I love the mother and all the children more than I can tell you. Also I would love to learn a lot—ever so many things. Nika and Agnes know so much and are so talented. I would like to learn to do everything they do. If you will let me stay I shall be immensely happy.

Give my greetings to Martha and Esther and Matthew.

Your Cornelli."

Mr. Hellmut shook his head as he folded the letters. "If that were really so!" he said to himself. "Less than two weeks ago they told me this child could not be trained, and I myself saw how obstinate and stubborn she was—and now! I certainly must not take quite literally what has probably been written on the spur of the moment." Nevertheless Mr. Hellmut was greatly pleased over the news and felt he was relieved of his greatest anxiety. Mrs. Halm was willing to take his daughter in hand, and she and her children had impressed him most favorably. How long they could get along with the obstinate child time alone would tell.

Mrs. Halm soon arranged matters so that Cornelli began a regular course of studies. Agnes insisted it was most important that she begin the study of music, and as Cornelli herself was eager to do so and was ambitious to do all that Nika and Agnes did she plunged into every branch of study that was opened to her.

Dino was now well again and had resumed his school course so every morning the four children started down the street and engaged in lively conversation until they separated to go to their different schools. If they met on their homeward journey, the conversation was still livelier for then they had their school experiences to relate. In this Cornelli always led them all, for she could depict every situation so vividly that all four would mount the stairs in gales of laughter.

Mux was the only one who was not happy these days. His playmate, Cornelli, had been lost to him, and in his anger he would call out to the laughing quartette as they came climbing up the stairs one behind the other, "If I owned the schools I would burn them all down!"

"But not all the teachers too, Mux!" said Dino. "If so one would have to tell even a worse tale about you than you told about Agnes."

Now the door between Cornelli's bedroom and

the one occupied by Nika and Agnes was always left open. All of them wished it so, and there was no longer a single evening when they did not make use of the very last moment to talk over the many things that interested all three.

Cornelli had nothing but admiration for Nika and all she did, and she could not understand how Nika who was so lovely and could do such wonderful things could have a sorrow. She thought about it a great deal because she knew by Nika's appearance that the girl must be bearing some secret grief. And she knew that Agnes too had hers for frequently in the happiest moments she would suddenly pause and say, "You may well be happy, Cornelli, for everything goes your way, but with us, ah!" and she would pucker her forehead in such a way that Cornelli was sure her sorrow gave her intense pain. She would have been so glad to help, but she refrained from asking what was causing the trouble, for she remembered how glad she had been when nobody had asked to know what was the matter with her.

One day Agnes came home from her music lesson flushed with excitement as never before. "Mama," she called out from the doorway, "the teacher has distributed the pieces we have to play for our examinations. Mine are the most difficult of all, and as he handed them over to me, he said: 'I shall make a real success out of you.' "

Then she tossed away her music sheets as though they were her greatest enemies and ran off to her room, threw herself into a chair and sobbed aloud.

Full of pity, Cornelli ran after her and putting her arms around her neck she said, "Oh, Agnes, I know just how it is when one has to cry. But why cry when your teacher has just praised you so?"

"But what is the use of praise?" Agnes burst out. "What good is it to me if I can play ever so well and if I would practice gladly day and night? It is all useless! Nika and I can only go on another year; then everything is over. She can't paint after that and I can't take music lessons. We have to become dressmakers and there will be no time to take the higher courses in school. I would a thousand times rather travel through the world singing in front of the houses for coppers—yes, I'd do that!"

"Can't your mother do anything to prevent

that?" asked Cornelli, remembering how Mrs. Halm had helped her in her great trouble.

"No, she can't do a thing, and she is unhappy about it. There is no one in the world who can help us since our guardian wishes it that way," declared Agnes, "and he says there is nothing else for us."

Cornelli was greatly depressed by this explanation, for now she understood why Nika often had such sad eyes; it really was a great sorrow and pierced Cornelli's heart. When Agnes had one of these fits of despair, it was several days before she recovered. Then Nika did not have a word to say, and the mother gazed quietly and sadly on her children. Dino also grew silent, for he knew the thoughts that tortured mother and sisters. How he would have loved to help them all, but he knew of no way! These days Cornelli could not laugh or recount the experiences of the day in her comic way for she knew only too well what it is to bear a heavy sorrow.

CHAPTER X

NEW LIFE IN ILLERBACH

WINTER had come, and the days were so filled with regular work for all the inhabitants of the attic apartment that every evening brought a general lamentation that there were not enough hours in the day. Agnes especially looked as if she could spit fire in her indignation when all activity had to be put aside and bedtime had come.

"One loses half one's life sleeping!" she often exclaimed when roused to speech. "If you would only allow us to sing right through the night, mama! We would be just that much more eager for our work next morning if we could sing to our hearts' content and not have to stop just when we are at our best."

But Mrs. Halm did not agree with this view at all, and the night hours were always given over to sleep.

Cornelli's singing was pure delight to Agnes. She sang everything easily, without effort, like a bird, and her voice was true and clear. There was no other contralto in the whole school so full and sure as hers, the teacher declared, and during class instruction he would choose Cornelli to lead the chorus.

In the middle of the winter Mr. Hellmut wrote to Mrs. Halm to say that since his daughter was so well taken care of he had decided to undertake a prolonged journey abroad. His last trip had been cut short in order not to bind his kind cousin to his house too long. He had intended to pay Cornelli a visit, but now found himself unable to do so because of his sudden decision.

It seemed that spring had never come as quickly as it did following this winter, or so thought Cornelli one day when she was released from school earlier than the other pupils and stepped out into the streets to find a warm wind blowing and the melted snow dripping from the roofs. On a sunny roof a little bird was singing, rejoicing at the blue sky above. Cornelli paused to listen as the bird continued to warble its pretty song. Cornelli's imagination carried her back to Illerbach: the young beech trees would be showing the first tender green of the new leaves; the early violets would be peeping from under the hedge, and in the garden by the house the yellow crocuses would be lifting their pretty heads, and all around the birds would be piping in the trees—it was home, so sweet! As she pictured it all, she ran along the street and then up the stairs in a fervor of excitement and, taking pen and ink, she seated herself and wrote:

"Dear Papa:

I am positive there is no more beautiful spot on earth than our home just now. May I not return soon? The violets must be in blossom and the woods all green. Soon the early flowers will spring up in our garden, and then the roses, then the berries. And the meadows will be blue with forget-me-nots. Oh, there is no place anywhere like our home! How I would like to show it all to Mrs. Halm, Nika and Agnes, and take Mux out to see the little kid. Dino has seen the garden and the meadows and he is longing to return to Illerbach. Oh, if I could only see it all again soon!

A hundred kisses from

Your daughter Cornelli."

Three weeks later an answer came. Her father wrote that his journey had been considerably longer than he had intended at first, and expressed great pleasure that Cornelli realized she had a beautiful home, but said he was unwilling for her to leave her school just now. She must remain in the city until the summer holidays; he himself would be abroad that long. But she had his permission to invite the entire Halm family, who had been so kind to her, to visit her for the holidays; there was plenty of room for them all in the house, and he, as well as Cornelli, was deeply grateful.

At first Cornelli was a little disappointed that it should be so many weeks before she was to see the plum garden, the meadows and the beech woods, for her desire had grown stronger day by day. But the prospect of having the entire family with her, including Dino and his mother, pleased her so much that her disappointment soon disappeared. Still greater was her joy when at dinner she told them of her father's invitation and saw the jubilation that broke out. The girls had had no hopes of an outing during the holidays, but had expected that they would have to spend this summer, as others, in the hot attic. And now to have the prospect of roaming the fields of lovely Illerbach, about which Dino could never talk enough! Added to this, they were to live in Cornelli's home and, according to Dino, both house and garden were the finest in all the world. Agnes shouted for joy, and Nika's face lighted up like a sunbeam. Their mother was quite overcome with ecstasy and gratitude. How often she had worried in secret about Dino! How she had longed to be able to send him to Illerbach long enough to regain his full vigor! Now the dear God suddenly took away not only all her cares, but turned them into the richest blessings.

Dino smiled in utter satisfaction and kept repeating, "You should just see how beautiful it all is! That garden! Those trees! Those horses! Oh, the whole Illerbach!"

There were still many days, even weeks, before that lovely time would arrive, but the prospect ahead of them all made the waiting time no great hardship.

For Cornelli matters were different. Her longing for her own home grew stronger, more passionate every day, and whenever she saw any little patch of green in the city, she pictured the house, the meadows and the trees at Illerbach. Her desire to look upon it all again, to be home once more, was so acute it gave her actual pain. It seemed as though the day would never come; that she would never see her home again. But come it did. The big trunk was put on the cart and the whole family followed it to the railroad station. Trine brought up the rear, wide-eyed in astonishment. Although she was now on the way, it was beyond her comprehension that she should be permitted to make a journey to the country. Cornelli had begged so earnestly for her that Mrs. Halm could not withstand her appeal, though she said Cornelli herself must be responsible for the unexpected guest.

At last they reached the station, boarded the train and were off to the country! The sun shone on field and meadow, and not a cloud flecked the blue. Cornelli sat by an open window and eagerly viewed the flying landscape. The two hours and more necessary for the journey passed quickly; now it was time to alight.

"There he comes! There he comes!" cried Cornelli, and darted to the road that led to the valley, where Matthew had just reined in his impatient bays.

Cornelli stood in front of them and shouted to the driver, "O Matthew, here I am home again! Is everything the same?"

"Welcome, Cornelli! Welcome home!" said

he, his face wreathed in smiles, for his master's child was his greatest pride. "But how you have grown, Cornelli! My, how you have changed!" And he shook her hand in his delight, then turned to open the carriage door, for the family had come up.

"Ah, here is our acquaintance, the young gentleman who was here last year," said Matthew as Dino stepped up to shake hands.

"But you looked very much better then, very much better!"

"I believe you, Matthew, for I had good milk from your stable and breathed in the fresh morning air then," said Dino.

Mrs. Halm had stepped into the carriage and the two girls quickly followed, but Mux stood staring at the two magnificent bays and it was with difficulty they drew him inside.

"We will take the horses with us," Matthew promised, for the youngster's undisguised admiration pleased him. "You can come out every day and look at them, and ride them down to the spring."

That prospect helped. Now they were all in the carriage. Trine had climbed up on the driver's seat beside Matthew and the coach rolled off down the valley.

"Mother, mother, look at the red daisies!" called Cornelli. "Look at the golden buttercups! Oh, see all those blue forget-me-nots!" She jumped up, for she could not sit still any longer, she had to gaze before her, behind her, on every side. The meadows had never been so full of flowers, and every moment brought a fresh shout of ecstasy. When the carriage drove into the courtyard, Cornelli was the first to jump out.

"Esther! Esther! How are you?" she called out to her old friend who, arrayed in a snow-white apron, came out to receive the guests in calm dignity.

"Now I am home again! Is everything just as it always was? Is the garden just the same? And Martha? And her cottage?"

"Yes, yes, Cornelli! And how are you?" replied Esther, watching Cornelli closely. "But you have changed! Good gracious, how you have changed! You are not the same girl!"

But Cornelli had run into the house, through the living-room, up to her own room. Everything was just the same as it had been! She darted out again to lead Mrs. Halm into the house, her face quite radiant with joy.

Mr. Hellmut was at his office, absorbed in his business, but when he heard the sound of wheels, said he to himself: "There they are already!" and tossing his office coat over the back of the chair, drew on his house coat, left the foundry and crossed over to the courtyard. "Oh, dear!" he sighed as he went, for there arose the memory of the impression his daughter had made on him when he returned from his journey a year ago, and she had stood before him so timid and shy, her eyes averted and looking like a South Sea Islander. "What will the child look like now?"

As he stepped into the living-room Cornelli

looked up at him, and involuntarily he paused in surprise at what he saw.

Cornelli now flew to his side, crying, "Oh, papa, papa! How lovely it is at home! And everything is just as it used to be. Oh, how happy I am to be home again!"

CORNELLI, HER CHILDHOOD

The father wanted to embrace his child, but held her off a moment to look at her again.

"Cornelli, my child, you look at me just as your mother used to do," he said, tears filling his eyes. "How does it come you have grown so like her?" he asked in deep emotion as he folded her in his arms. "How have you changed so? Tell me, how did it all come about?"

"Mother knows, papa. Mother helped me," explained Cornelli, her eyes beaming with joy as she led Mrs. Halm forward.

Mr. Hellmut advanced to meet her and said in his courteous manner as he greeted one after the other, "A hearty welcome to our house, Mrs. Halm, a hearty welcome to both you and your children!" Then, taking Cornelli by the hand, he continued in a voice that showed his agitation, "See what you have brought back to me! What have you done to my child, and how did you do it? Can she be the same child I took to you?" He kept gazing at Cornelli. Was it really she, or just an imaginary creature?

Faithful Esther was carrying in the dishes to set the dining table and standing in the doorway informed her master the rooms for the guests were in readiness and suggested that perhaps the ladies would like to withdraw to them before the meal.

Mrs. Halm and her daughters gladly accepted but Cornelli said, "I may run over to Martha's, may I not, papa? I will be back soon."

When Mr. Hellmut nodded assent, Dino begged to go along; he could not remain behind when it was a matter of visiting Martha.

Martha had heard that Cornelli was expected, and that she was bringing her friends with her as guests, so she had been intently watching the courtyard and garden for any sign of Cornelli or perhaps of Dino. Now both came running up the steps. Martha hurried out. That was Dino, just as she had known him! But Cornelli—Martha gazed on the child, pressed her hands and tried to say something, but the tears ran down her cheeks and she could not utter one word.

"O Martha, I am so happy to be back home and I've run over at once to see you!" Cornelli exclaimed. "Are you not glad with me? Oh, I'm so happy! I'm so happy!"

"I too! Oh, I certainly am!" Martha assured her. "My joy at the memories you awoke overcame me. You look exactly like your mother.

CORNELLI, HER CHILDHOOD

How different you look than when you went away, Cornelli! God has blessed your stay in the city. To me it is wonderful. Oh, how I have prayed for this!"

Then she had to shake Dino's hand, but her pleasure in greeting him was mixed with sadness. "Why so thin and pale, Dino?" she asked anxiously. "You were much stouter a year ago."

"That is why I have come back to Illerbach," answered Dino cheerfully, "and you must rejoice with us, Mrs. Wolf, for we are immensely happy to be back again, Cornelli and I. Everything here is just as lovely as it was a year ago, and we will visit you every day, for I feel quite at home here."

Martha could not speak from sheer emotion. There stood Cornelli before her as fresh and joyful as ever. All the sadness and the disfigurement had vanished from her face, and the joyousness which had taken their place stirred kind old Martha's heart. That was the way the girl's young mother used to look. And there stood Dino gay and smiling as ever, assuring her of the warmth of his friendship. She could hardly believe all this happiness was hers.

"We have to go now, Martha," said Cornelli, "but you know how it used to be when I came running over to you every day, and I will do so again."

"And I with her! I with her!" exclaimed Dino, and as she watched them trip down the steps tears of joy dimmed Martha's eyes, yet she watched them until they were lost from sight. Even after they had disappeared she stood gazing, with folded hands, and murmured quietly, "O Lord, my heart is brimming over with gratitude. Thou hast turned to blessing everything that was hard for the child. All has been for her good!"

As the children stepped into the house, Cornelli said, "Go in, Dino; I'll come directly," and she turned into the kitchen.

"Just as I thought! Our Cornelli soon had to find her way into the kitchen," smiled Esther with satisfaction. "Come, Cornelli, let me have a good look at you," and she stepped directly in front of the child. "You have grown some during the year and now how neat and trim you look! Yes, it gives one pleasure to look at our Cornelli now!"

Cornelli blushed slightly, for she remembered

how she looked when she went away, how difficult she had been and how she had resisted
everyone's kindly interest in her.

"Esther, I want to tell you something. Where
is Trine, the maid I brought along?" she asked.

"I told her to go out and look at the vegetable
garden," said Esther. "She kept standing in
my way in the kitchen. She does not seem over-
bright."

"No, that she certainly is not, but look here,
Esther. I want to tell you something about
Trine. You will be kind to her, won't you?" she
pleaded. "You see Trine is awkward and
stupid, but she can't help it. Perhaps you do not
know how that is, but I know very well. And if
you are real kind to her she won't mind it so
much. You will do me that favor, won't you?"

Esther gazed in astonishment at Cornelli as
she ran to the dining-room. "Where does the
child get such ideas?" she asked herself. "One
would suppose our Cornelli had had a humble
start in life instead of being Mr. Hellmut's
daughter, who can have everything she wants,"
and she continued to shake her head.

After the first merry meal the children were
told to run out into the garden. They already

knew all there was to be seen there. How enthusiastically Dino had described the garden with its wealth of flowers of every color, its trellises of blushing peaches, the laden pear and apple trees, the great stables beyond with the glossy cows and the magnificent horses. Now they were to see all these things and all five dashed off.

Mr. Hellmut tarried over his black coffee, and Mrs. Halm was glad to keep him company.

"Now, Mr. Hellmut," she said as the door closed behind the children, "allow me to thank you from the bottom of my heart for your great kindness."

"What? How? *You* wish to thank *me?*" he interrupted. "Permit me to say a word! How can I ever repay the debt I owe you? See what you have done for my daughter! How well you have trained her! How fully she is transformed! I have to gaze at her time and again to be sure it is really so. How did you do it, and how can I ever thank you for the trouble, pains and patience it must have taken to bring her back to me like this?"

"No, Mr. Hellmut, the matter does not stand that way at all," declared Mrs. Halm. "Cornelli has given me no trouble, and her training did not require much patience. If by love I was able to bring out her good qualities and help in the delightful development, that is all that I have done. Cornelli has never given me a trying moment. We all had grown so fond of the child that it was painful to think the time was near when she would have to leave us. I shall never forget how she entertained my Dino during his sickness, not to mention my little son with her unending merriment and kindness. Yes, Mr. Hellmut, you have a lovely child."

In his agitation Mr. Hellmut leaped to his feet and paced to and fro, but it was a far different emotion than that which, just a year ago, had driven him to stride up and down that same room.

"You do not know how much this means to me, Mrs. Halm," he said as he stood before her. "You do not know how you are freeing me from torture. I have suffered self-accusations that I neglected my Cornelia's child until it was too late, until she had grown hopelessly obstinate. Now you bring her back to me, and I see the likeness of her mother in her eyes, her expression, her whole appearance. And you tell me she is merry and kind by nature. That is my Cornelia over again; she was just like that."

"I would like to correct another of your views, Mr. Hellmut," Mrs. Halm continued. "I am persuaded the first few years of a child's life are most important. Cornelli needed the loving guidance of a mother. Nevertheless, I must say she was by no means a neglected child when she came to me. From all I can gather from her and from Dino, who lived a summer with the good Martha, I believe that that good woman has given your child the best that we can give children in education of the soul. I hold Mrs. Martha in high esteem; she thoroughly understands childhood."

"That is what my Cornelia used to say, and that is why I had such faith in her. But the time came when I thought everything had gone wrong and I did not correctly estimate what she meant to the child. You have reminded me of my indebtedness—"

Such shouts of joy resounded from the garden that they both stepped to the open window and heard Mux scream: "Mama, mama! Look! A real goat-boy and a real goat!"

Sure enough, Mux was sitting in a pretty

CORNELLI, HER CHILDHOOD

little wicker carriage, a pair of reins in one hand and a whip in the other, while a slender little goat drew the carriage. Agnes and Cornelli ran on either side for protection, while Dino kept a check on the reins so the goat could not run away. All the children shouted with joy over the wonderful ride.

Mux screamed out his rapture to his mother for he was quite beside himself. She really had to see all this grandeur close by, so she came out, and Mr. Hellmut with her, though he went off in another direction. Soon afterward he climbed the steps to the little veranda where Martha sat at her mending.

"Mr. Hellmut!" she exclaimed in surprise and, rising, she opened the door and led him into the cottage, for there was not room for two people on the little porch.

"Martha," he began in his most businesslike manner, much to her astonishment, "I have ruined your business and that calls for compensation. I have made your boarder desert you for all time. So I have just purchased your cottage from yonder farmer, together with the little piece of land in front of it. There you will find a little more room for your carnations, and with good management the rent you will save will make your days much pleasanter. Is that satisfactory?"

"Oh, Mr. Hellmut! This cottage my own, and a garden besides? Oh, Mr. Hellmut!" But he would not allow her to say more, and after a hearty handshake hurried off.

CORNELLI, HER CHILDHOOD

The large red raspberries peeped from under the green leaves, and already the golden yellow plums were falling from the overburdened tree. Mux revelled in uninterrupted joy from morning until evening. Even before his eyes were quite open in the morning he would cry out to his mother in alarm, "Mother, are we still here? Haven't we gone away yet?" Then began the daylight hours, each more lovely than the last; Mux did not know which was best.

Mrs. Halm had a real stable suit made for him, for the boy did not only go in and out of the stable, but often spent the whole day in the barn.

Matthew had become his best friend, and was always thinking up some amusement for him for he took a great liking to the boy because of his special interest in farming. If Matthew had to undertake some work that did not permit Mux's presence, he always discovered something for him to do elsewhere. "While I am busy, go over to the raspberry bushes," he would say. "No, not those up there. Down there are the finest, largest berries because the sun has thoroughly ripened them. Then rest under the plum tree until I come."

When Matthew was not to be found and Dino
and Cornelli were busy with their own plans,
Mux had still another friend who always gave
him a hearty reception. He wandered off to
Esther when she was in the vegetable garden,
where new and pleasant things awaited him for
here green peas, which at home were served
only on feast days, grew in such abundance that
they weighed the vines down in a wonderful
way, and he grew quite anxious when he looked
on as Esther picked a great basketful. When
he said in warning, "Don't take them all at once
or we will not have any left for another time,"
she just laughed and said, "They'll keep on
growing and in a week there'll be a lot more."

From the vegetable garden Mux tagged
Esther to the kitchen, where he also gained much
useful knowledge. No pastry ever came to the
table that he could not tell how it was made; and
he also knew just how it tasted. These were
happy days for Mux.

No less were they for the other children. Dino
and Cornelli had started a great enterprise:
they laid out Martha's garden after an original
plan, and had so much to do that the two were
never to be found, much as Agnes fought with

Dino for a share of Cornelli's time. But Dino always came out winner, and Cornelli went with him. He had been her first friend, therefore she remained steadfastly true to him. Agnes found comfort in the fact that she could sit at the lovely piano at any time, and just as long as she wished. And then, too, every evening she could sing with Cornelli, for she was always at home then. Mr. Hellmut would seat himself in his armchair, and then the singing began. He could not have too many songs. And from time to time he would say to Mrs. Halm with shining eyes, "The child has her mother's voice except that the mother's was fuller as well as softer."

Then Mrs. Halm's face would light up with joy as she replied: "Just a little patience, Mr. Hellmut! Some day you will find there is nothing further to wish for in Cornelli's voice."

Nika was transformed; no shadow now darkened her face. In silent happiness she wandered with her paints from one beautiful spot in the garden to another. Then up into the beechwood, and on up to the heights where stood the great oak with the bench beneath, where she sat down and gazed on house and garden and far

off down the green valley below. There Nika
tarried long hours at a time, bending over her
pleasing work, then dreaming, and then returning to her canvas, finding complete happiness in
the thought that no one came to disturb her, no
uncongenial tasks awaited her.

Mrs. Halm watched the glow of health returning to Dino's cheeks and the joyous faces
of her daughters, but in spite of her rejoicing
the thought would intrude: How different it
will all be again when these days come to an end
and life in the little rooms must be taken up
again under the threatening shadows of the
coming years!

The holiday period was approaching its end
but no one had much time to think about it for
Mr. Hellmut's birthday was coming and was to
be celebrated with a great fete. Mrs. Halm had
planned that each of the children should think
out some surprise for the occasion; each one was
to be left to his own device. Little Mux alone
was told to memorize a pretty poem of congratu-
lation that his mother had written. It required
a long time and much pains to persuade the short
verse to stay in his little head for it was so filled
with thoughts about barns and stables, kitchens

nd goat-carts, plums, bugs and ants, that it as hardly able to hold anything more.

Nika needed no advice, for she had long since etermined what she would do, and immediately fter a meal would disappear.

Agnes and Cornelli bolted the door of the music room, but mysterious music floated out.

Only Dino remained undecided about his problem and time and again when alone with his mother and Mux inquired, "What can I do, mother?"

"Draw a picture of the pretty goat," suggested Mux.

"Oh, you goat-boy Mux!" exclaimed Dino. But while rejecting the suggestion of a goat picture, he did receive an idea from Mux, for he suddenly called out much pleased, "I will draw the two bays. I'll show one walking, the other trotting. Matthew must lead them up and down before me."

He ran off to the stable and from that day forward he had many secret engagements with Matthew.

At last the birthday arrived. When Mr. Hellmut stepped into the dining-room for breakfast he was enticed into the adjoining room by the lovely song that Agnes and Cornelli were singing in honor of his day. He only patted both the girls on the back with fatherly tenderness, then went into the dining-room but they knew it was because he was unable to speak. Here Mux met him and repeated his congratulatory verses without a falter. Two pictures lay on the table before him. They were of his bays; he knew them in an instant, and he was so pleased that he did not put them down for quite a little while. But then something else caught his eye. In the middle of the table, so large that it had to be carefully supported, stood a painting of his house, the garden, the meadows beyond with a far view of the valley and the distant blue mountains in the rich coloring so true to nature. Mr. Hellmut stood dumbfounded before it, for that was the view he had loved from earliest childhood.

"Cornelli, come here!" her father called. "Look at this picture. Don't you love it just as your father does?"

"Oh, yes, I love it, papa! I love it so much!" declared Cornelli, "and each day I think I never knew how beautiful it is until I went far away from it."

"Ah, Cornelli, if only you did not have this lovely home!" exclaimed Agnes passionately as she stood behind her.

"Why, Agnes, why say such a thing?" said her shocked mother, while Mr. Hellmut gazed in astonishment at Agnes who was regarding the painting with fiery eyes.

"So you two have had an out-and-out quarrel and you wish Cornelli did not have such a lovely home?" he said, hiding a smile.

Agnes flushed painfully and said, "Oh, no! I did not mean that, Mr. Hellmut; certainly not! Neither have I quarreled with Cornelli, though I have with Dino because he always wants her for himself. But if Cornelli did not have this lovely home, and if, like me, she had to give up her music lessons and earn her living, we two could get along beautifully because she has such a fine voice. Between us we could hire a harp and travel to strange cities and sing before the houses. Then later we could give concerts and establish a school of music. But alone I can do nothing—absolutely nothing!"

Mrs. Halm's blood ran cold at her daughter's outbreak which no look or sign from her could check. Agnes's eyes still gleamed like fire in the intensity of her unusually passionate excitement.

"I am in favor of the singing school," said Mr. Hellmut quite seriously, "but above all I am in favor of sitting down to breakfast. I hope the usual chocolate is to be served today, for it is a good old birthday custom that we should not neglect. Well, a singing school ought to be established," he continued when all were finally seated and Mux had viewed with huge satisfaction the three kinds of cakes which were served with the three big chocolate pots. "The wandering harp performers are a little too poetical for my taste; on the other hand, the singing school idea pleases me. I would like to have a share in it, and to have it built on my estate. Over in the foundry there are a number of workers who have children. The mothers have more than enough to do with the housekeeping and their smallest ones. Let Agnes and Cornelli establish a singing school in Illerbach, and all the children whose mothers have no time for singing can go. When the children arrive they will be served with a bowl of bread and milk to make their voices fuller. That gives us the singing school! At intervals I will have both

242

teachers pursue further studies so that they will progress themselves.

"I have also found work for Nika; she shall fill my house from top to bottom with paintings and so that she may gain new ideas as well as inspiration I will send her to the city to study with her master.

"Dino shall help me give my two bays exercise, and he must begin by learning to ride them. That will do both horses and boy good. And I can make special use of Mux, for he shall become the manager of my estate. The good start he has made in the knowledge of agriculture with Matthew and Esther will be continued as long as the fields are green and the trees bear fruit. And the mother is to remain with us to take care of us all. Now tell me, does the proposition meet with your approval? Shall we have it thus?"

Absolute silence reigned. The children hardly dared confess they had understood his words, and Mrs. Halm was so overcome with emotion that she could not restrain the tears. Could it be possible? Could it be that her many burdens, her deep griefs were to be suddenly lifted? Might she believe it?

Then Mux shouted in a loud voice, "Yes, we will!" for it was quite clear to him that Mr. Hellmut's proposition meant that he would keep on doing the pleasant things with Matthew and Esther.

Mr. Hellmut burst out laughing and said, "Then the leading voice is in my favor! Mrs. Halm, let us divide between us, but I confess right away I want the larger half. Suppose you retain the oversight of the children during the winter, arrange their courses of study and all, but in the summer let me have them with me to enjoy the result of all their progress. That will also give me the advantage of having you to keep my household in order. Is that satisfactory, or do I ask too big a share?"

Mrs. Halm had gained control of her emotions and now reaching out her hand which still trembled in agitation she said, "Oh, Mr. Hellmut, how can I ever thank you? I do not know how to give expression to all that is in my heart, or how to thank you for such boundless benevolence! You cannot know what your generosity means to us all!"

Now the children began to realize that this almost unbelievable good fortune was actually

244

true. Nika ran to Mr. Hellmut with sparkling eyes and seized his hand, but she could find no words to tell her gratitude. Agnes hurried up behind her, but Dino succeeded in claiming second place, and Mr. Hellmut found it impossible to grasp all the proffered hands at once. As Mux found it impossible to reach his benefactor, he climbed up behind his chair, threw both his arms around Mr. Hellmut's neck and shouted many thousand thanks right into his ears. The sounds of rejoicing grew louder and louder.

"Cornelli," said her father at last, "carry our thanks to your foster-mother; to her is due all this gratitude, for it was Mrs. Halm who brought all this happiness to our house."

This Cornelli did from the bottom of her heart, for she realized all Mrs. Halm had done for her. Then, suddenly, as though seized with the same thought, Dino and Cornelli rushed off. They could wait no longer to carry the great news to Martha; there was nobody in the world who could share their intense joy as she could.

Their aged friend received the announcement with an overflow of happiness, and as tears ran down her cheeks, she kept repeating, "Oh, Cornelli, didn't the good Lord do well for you—far

CORNELLI, HER CHILDHOOD

better than we knew how to ask? We ought
always to leave all to Him, to place everything
in His hands. We will all our lives long, will
we not, Cornelli?"

Cornelli nodded assent; she had not forgotten
how she had complained to Martha, and how
Martha had directed her to seek help from God;
how the good woman had said that if matters do
not shape themselves as we wish, nevertheless
they are always for our highest good. How
much better the outcome was than Cornelli had
ever been able to wish!

Such rejoicing had never sounded in the Hellmut house before as Agnes started when she and
Nika went to their room that night. Cornelli
had come to their door for her usual bedtime
visit, and found Agnes hopping about the room
like a bird just escaped from captivity and rejoicing, "No more troubles! No more fears for
the future! Just happy songs to our hearts'
content! Oh, to spend every summer here with
you, Cornelli! We are the happiest people in
all the whole world, and you have brought it
about, Cornelli, you incomparable Cornelli!"
And seizing Cornelli's hand, the two danced
around the room until Nika warned her sister

that Mr. Hellmut might rue his invitation if
their stay began with such an uproar, though,
truth to tell, she herself looked as though she
would not be a whit sorry to join in the dance.
When the two had subsided on the bed, she continued, "Surely, Cornelli, the day you entered
our house was the most blessed one of the entire
year. Let us celebrate it every year as the
greatest festival in this house."

247

Of late Nika had been so friendly, even so affectionate toward her that Cornelli had been very happy about it, but it was almost past belief she should speak like this.

When the news of the protracted stay of the Halm family and their return each summer reached the kitchen, Esther said, "Good! That pleases me better than if some other people I know were to come again. It is better for me, for Cornelli and the entire house."

"Oh, if only I could come again!" sighed Trine, who always wore a smiling face these days. "Oh, how happy one feels here!"

"That's very true," Esther agreed. "And I don't know why you shouldn't come. Don't you worry, Trine! When Cornelli and I take any one under our protection, I would like to know why she should not come again!"

As the days passed Mr. Hellmut was less and less in favor of permitting the Halms to leave, especially for so long a time. "Mrs. Halm," he proposed at last, "suppose this year we extend the children's stay in the country until late in the fall. Dino, for whom study is of the greatest importance, is least able to return to the city. It is absolutely necessary for him to regain his full health and strength. If special instruction is required, we can always call in our good Mr. Mallinger."

Mrs. Halm was of the same opinion, and unspeakably grateful to Mr. Hellmut for making such an arrangement for her son possible.

"Then, again, there is another reason for prolonging your stay," continued Mr. Hellmut. "It is my desire to pay you and your children a visit now and then during the winter. But climbing the stairs to your apartment under the roof would be rather difficult for me, so I have rented a comfortable dwelling for you which will be ready in the late fall. I hope this does not displease you, though it does involve extra work. So a little additional rest is quite necessary that you go to your task with full vigor."

"I can but thank you—always keep thanking you," said Mrs. Halm, but further words were impossible just then as all the children came storming upon them as Cornelli had just told them of her father's intention to keep them in Illerbach until winter.

When the fruit in the orchard had ripened under the autumn sun, Matthew stood at the stable door watching Dino and Cornelli shake one tree and then another, while the other children scrambled after the falling fruit, biting first into a luscious apple and then into a juicy pear. He rubbed his hands with pleasure and said with a smile, "Things are different from a year ago! Now there are no decaying plums, no forgotten pears in the orchard!"

The songs that floated out of the Hellmut house every evening were songs of praise and gratitude that were lifted to Heaven in sincere rejoicing, and more than once as Mr. Hellmut kissed his little daughter good-night he would say smilingly, "Is it not true, Cornelli, that the good Lord meant well for us when He gave our aged Martha the idea of writing such an inviting notice for the newspaper?"

THE END

Neil L.
Ehmke

June 1931